S0-BHW-070

ONLY FOR
A YEAR

ONLY FOR
A YEAR

•

Ludima Gus Burton

AVALON BOOKS
NEW YORK

PRINTED IN THE UNITED STATES OF AMERICA
ON ACID-FREE PAPER
BY HADDON CRAFTSMEN, BLOOMSBURG, PENNSYLVANIA

Dedicated to the memory of my beloved husband,
my wonderful, supportive family and the
fabulous Saratoga Romance Writers Chapter.

Chapter One

There he was, coming out of the elevator—the big, rugged man of her fantasy.

It didn't matter that Brent Chambers, owner of the company where she worked as a computer clerk, hardly knew she existed. It didn't matter that she had vowed never to fall in love again. Hadn't her beloved Johnny died and left her alone and brokenhearted? Never would she be foolish enough to open her heart again to risk pain and anguish. But fantasies could be woven at will. In fantasies, love lasted forever, happiness reigned and security was hers.

Sarah Victoria Gordan stood in her cramped computer cubicle, looking at her employer over a forest of four-foot high dividers. Forgotten were the reports for which her supervisor waited.

An aura of command swirled around him. His shoulders looked broad enough to carry any load and filled his tailored dark suit jacket. His trousers, with their razor-sharp creases, hugged his thighs. Thick black brows arched over intelligent eyes. He glowered at the report in his hand. The tanned fingers of his

1

other hand tunneled through his jet black hair, wreaking havoc with the stylized haircut. He shrugged his shoulders and looked up—right at her, as though no dividers, cubicles or other employees existed. Just the two of them.

His gaze held her captive for an earth-stopping moment. Awareness surged between them, tantalizing and tingling. His secretary walked toward him. The spell broke.

Her knees suddenly weak, Sarah sank into her chair, lost from view in the maze of cubicles.

Hard to believe it had happened again.

After watching him from afar for a year, she had made physical contact with him last week. It had happened as she was hurrying down the hall. She bumped, full-tilt, into his hard chest. The files in her hand flew in all directions.

"Oh, I'm so sorry—I wasn't looking—"

"It's all right. Let me help you."

Sarah, her cheeks burning with embarrassment, didn't look into the face that was so close to hers. When he knelt to pick up the files, his spicy cologne wafted to her. His shoulders brushed hers. Her heart thundered and her breathing was swift and shallow. Her fingers trembled but she held on to the recovered papers he laid into them. Task accomplished, they stood up. She tipped back her head and a traitorous warm rush of feeling threatened to spill out of her.

As though sensing her feelings, surprise leaped into his blue eyes. His speculative, intent gaze lasted but a moment. He shook his head and hurried away from her.

Sarah had scurried to her station and taken deep breaths. She had imagined his reaction. Only *she* had been affected. Only *her* toes had curled in her shoes. Only *her* heart had been grabbed by a fist.

Today his gaze had done it again—curled toes and all.

Her compatriot in the next cubicle interrupted her thoughts.

"Sarah, quick, grab some papers and stand up. Look who's heading for the boss's office. She's here again."

Sarah stood up and cautiously turned her body so she could see.

Brent Chambers's fiancée strode from the elevator toward his office, head held high and not looking to the right or the left. Wheat-colored hair fell in swirls about her shoulders. A black silk pant suit hugged the curves of her body. Heavy gold bracelets circled her right wrist and gold-hooped earrings swung from her ears. A breath-taking vision in black and gold.

In unison, Debbie and Sarah looked down at their drab attire and a simultaneous, envious sigh filled the air.

"She's so beautiful," Debbie said.

"A golden goddess," Sarah agreed. "And we'd better get back to work. I see Mrs. Backman frowning. We'll talk at lunch."

"Mmm, Elfredo makes the best brownies in the world." Debbie chewed happily.

"Can't be beat." Sarah licked her fingers. "What a figure Ashley Kirkland has." Sarah sighed. Her five feet, three inches were far short of Miss Kirkland's statuesque model height. Straight brown hair didn't attract attention, either. "Wonder what it would be like to have the money to buy an outfit like hers, or those bracelets."

"Bet they're twenty-four carat gold and not just gold-plated like ours."

"You'll probably call me crazy, but she doesn't look happy to me. I've never seen her smile at anyone, even Mr. Chambers. Having a man like him should have her grinning with delight."

"Yeah, you know those society dames—all haughty disdain."

"I think he deserves better than an ice maiden."

"It's his choice. He must see things in her we don't." Debbie laughed. "After all, we only see her walk in and walk out. And now we're the experts!"

"You're right. None of our business." Though it wasn't her concern, Sarah thought Ashley Kirkland, with her nose in the air and her icy aloofness, wasn't the woman who would make Brent Chambers happy. Sarah held her tongue. Only in her fantasies did she control Brent Chambers' happiness by making him her Prince Charming.

"To change the subject," Debbie said, "Are you going to ask for your evaluation tomorrow?"

Sarah straightened her shoulders and lifted her chin. "I sure am, even if I shake in my boots. There shouldn't be anything in my evaluation to keep me from getting my raise."

Not wanting personnel to shoulder the unpleasant task, Brent Chambers had decided to see his employees personally and tell them the unhappy news.

When Sarah was ushered into his office instead of being seen by the head of personnel, she looked down at her baggy suit coat. She recalled the couturie attire of his fiancée the day before, and cringed.

"What do you mean I don't get my raise?" Sarah's lips trembled. She sat up, her back rigid as a steel rod and clenched her hands. It had taken courage to ask Mr. Chambers for the raise in spite of her ill-fitting suit. How she wished she had worn her new spring outfit today.

"After a year, I'm entitled to it." She stared through her large black-rimmed glasses at Brent Chambers. Her brown eyes, flecked with gold, seemed to throw daggers at him.

"I'm sorry, Miss . . ." Brent Chambers, distracted by the beauty of her large eyes, with their long lashes, glanced down to read the name on her personnel folder lying on the large blotter of his neat desk. "Miss Gordan, but I've had to change company policy on merit raises at this time."

"But I've been counting on this raise!"

His dark blue eyes clashed with Sarah's at her third protest. Her heart fluttered and her breath became shallow but she didn't flinch.

"Your evaluation is excellent. It's nothing personal, I assure you."

Nothing personal? Of course it wasn't to him. He didn't even know her name!

"I'm sorry," he continued, "When business picks up, I'll do another review—perhaps in three months—"

"But I need it now!"

After this last outburst, his black eyebrows rose in displeasure and he pursed his lips.

Sarah became aware, at last, that he might fire her for her impertinence. She was surprised, however, to see the anger fade. The uncomfortable moment passed. His speculative gaze raked her from head to foot, making her nerve endings feel like they were rubbed with sand paper. She held her defiant stance for what seemed like an eternity and waited for his next words. She sensed he had made a decision.

"Instead of a raise, I have another proposition." He paused and then said softly, "I want you to marry me."

All breath swooshed out of Sarah's lungs. She gasped for air and then swallowed convulsively. Shock made her tremble. Had she heard correctly?

"Did you just ask me to mar-marry you? I don't even know you—I don't love you!"

"I know that. Love doesn't enter into this proposal. Well, yes, it does but—" Brent broke off, helpless to explain. He tried again, "This would be a marriage of convenience lasting for one year."

"I don't understand. You aren't making any sense." Sarah stood up and headed for the door. She didn't want any part of this bewildering interview.

Brent bounded out of his seat and stood in front of her. "Please wait. I have to find a woman to be my wife since my fiancée eloped with another man yesterday."

"Ashley Kirkland did that?" Sarah gasped. *The woman was a fool*!

"Yes." Brent's answer was curt. "Her unexpected action has created serious difficulties for me. Because I've reached my limit on all my credit resources, I need my inheritance money. I have to marry in order to get it on the fifteenth of May. Please sit down and let me explain."

Sarah sat at the edge of her chair. Heart-stopping wonder at his proposal and curiosity about the whole matter kept her from running out of the office. "I'm listening."

At that moment, Brent realized that he wanted Sarah Victoria Gordan to be the one to help him. He recalled how she caused his heart to quicken and his blood to rush to his head at every brief encounter he had with her—whether it was nodding to her in the lobby or running into her, full-tilt, in the hall, or looking into each other's eyes from across the room. He tried to forget the one night she had haunted his dreams. She had floated at the foot of his bed, clothed in a diaphanous white gown. Her big, cinnamon brown eyes, fringed with heavy lashes, laughed at him from behind dark-rimmed glasses. Her hair—very straight, with gold highlights the color of her eyes,—swung like a soft cloud around her shoulders. He wanted to catch it in his hands, to bury his face in it. But she disappeared when he attempted to touch her. And he called himself a fool for dreaming about an employee.

He had to convince her that only she could help him.

"This will be a business arrangement, a marriage only on paper."

Sarah stared at him, unable to utter a word.

Last night, still reeling from the shock of Ashley's elopement, he had realized that he and Ashley hadn't loved each other. Though he felt betrayed, he didn't have a broken heart. Had they married, it wouldn't have been the marriage of love his uncle wanted for him and so specified in his will. Hence, marrying someone else without being in love wouldn't be any different. Since he no longer had Ashley to marry, a marriage of convenience with another woman, secretly entered into for a year, was the only way to solve his problem by the deadline.

Each partner had to benefit. He would be getting a fortune and his family mansion. Big benefits for him.

But what would he offer the woman? A big lump sum, living in luxury for a year, an amiable divorce and alimony until she remarried? That might do it.

He drew up a prenuptial contract. Not what his Uncle Matthew intended, but he was desperate to save his company.

He thought about this woman he had to find. She didn't have to be a raving beauty, but a pleasing physical appearance was a must. He was going to see her first thing in the morning and the last thing at night. No older than his thirty-three years or younger than twenty-one. A stranger to his social circle. A quiet, calm and intelligent person who was a good listener and a woman of few words. Pliable to his needs and the demands of his business. A good actress. One who would honorably abide by the terms of their contract.

He was asking for the impossible—a perfect wife for his marriage of convenience.

Remembering his thoughts of last night, he took a deep breath and controlled the tremor in his hand. He pushed the contract across the desk toward Sarah. So much was riding on her acceptance. She fitted enough of his requirements to be asked to fill the role of his contract wife.

"This is what I'm offering. As you can see, you will benefit from this marriage as well as I."

He watched as Sarah read it through. Her eyes opened wide and a gasp escaped her. She read through it once more and shook her head from side to side.

"This . . . much? This lump sum—it's four times my yearly salary! Payable in monthly installments—

and you want me to live in your house, all expenses paid? Even alimony until I remarry after the divorce?"

"I wanted to be sure that you wouldn't lose anything by the sacrifice of your freedom for a year. I gain much more than you." He shuffled some papers on his desk into an untidy pile. "There is one other thing."

"I knew there was a catch. What do you really want from me?"

"I told you this wouldn't be a real marriage. We'll live together, but not as husband and wife. However, you'll have to pretend that you love me, and I, you. The world must believe we're marrying for love."

"Pretend I love you and you love me? Are you crazy?" Sarah took a shuddering breath. "This is to be a business arrangement. Why all this love stuff?"

Brent rotated his stiff shoulders. Sarah looked at his tousled hair. Sometime during the meeting he had loosened his tie and unbuttoned the top of his white shirt. He looked like a harried man. She wanted to smooth his hair back into place and tell him not to worry so much. She'd—whoa! He didn't need her to mother him. He just wanted to marry her in order to get his money. No tender feelings about this deal.

"Before my Uncle Matthew died, he confided his regrets for not marrying and giving me the family life he thought I deserved."

"But you were happy with him, weren't you?"

"In his quiet way, he loved me and taught me everything I know about business. When I started my own company, he was so proud. I can't lose it." The desperation in Brent's voice struck Sarah's heart. She knew what it was like to struggle for a goal and then see it taken away.

"When I learned the terms of the will, I understood

our last talks before he died. He tried to make sure I married for love and had a family—that I would never reach old age with the same regrets he had."

"But you don't love me. What you propose won't be following his wishes." For a fleeting moment Sarah thought how great would have been her happiness if he did it for love . . .

"I'm desperate. I have to marry in less than two weeks. My immediate priority is saving my company. After this year, I'll find a woman to love as Uncle Matthew wanted me to do."

Was Brent warning her that she would never be this woman? That he wanted her for only one reason? Why did this hurt?

"So you're asking me to help you to get around the will?"

"It's only for a year. When we're in public, we'll act the part of a loving couple. Just pretend you love me. Marital intimacy will not be forced upon you, I promise. In private, we will be only friends."

"What you're proposing is an impossibility. For a whole year we pretend we love each other? That this is a real love marriage?" Sarah shook her head. "I'm no actress and I abhor lying. And what do I tell my parents and brother?"

The possible failure of his plans stared Brent in the face. He tried another tack. "Please think before you refuse me. If I don't get my operating money on May fifteenth, I'll immediately have to scale back my work force. You and your co-workers would have to be considered in this move."

His words, spoken with authority, turned Sarah cold with dread. Not only had she been refused a raise, she could soon join the ranks of the unemployed. Unless, that is, she played her part. Brent's next words were an added surprise.

"I'll also lose my family home."

"Your house is in danger, too? How much more haven't you told me about your uncle's infamous will?" Sarcasm laced her question, to be overcome with sympathy. Lose his home? How terrible. And she could prevent this tragedy if she would only marry him.

The flush covering his face and the tightening of his lips showed how uncomfortable Brent was with his disclosures.

"That's all of it."

Sarah got up and paced back and forth before Brent's desk. In a nutshell, if she didn't agree to this marriage of convenience, his company could fail and he would lose his house.

And she'd be out of a job.

But why was she his only option? Surely he could find another woman he actually knew to do it. Heavens, the money alone was enough to tempt a woman.

"Why did you pick me for your scheme? You must have a list—"

"I don't. I only learned yesterday Ashley had left and gone to Paris. Since that time I've worked on my accounts to see if I could pull the company out of its trouble without the available inheritance money. No way. To find a wife by resorting to the want ads or the Internet is out of the question. When you asked for this interview, it seems like fate decreed this. You do need money . . ."

A delicate pink flush of discomfort covered Sarah's face. If she hadn't asked for the raise, he wouldn't know this fact. Nor would he ask her to be his partner-in-crime. Nor would she live in his house with him for a long year . . . Nor could she dream that the fates would work a miracle of love in her life again.

She left her chair and went to look out the big plate glass window. To save Brent, she would also be benefiting herself. But what about the changes in her life? Marriage, even in name only, to an attractive, virile man like Brent, was sure to be fraught with danger—heart-breaking danger. She hadn't missed the way he looked at her—nor could she ignore her own runaway feelings.

To see him every day and pretend she loved him? An impossible situation—especially when she could so easily fall in love with him. Besides, could he truly kiss her and be devoid of feeling?

She turned around and stared at him, hoping he couldn't read her thoughts.

Brent smiled at her and tried again, "We can do it. It's only for a short year. We're two intelligent adults—"

"Let me think."

"Please, don't refuse me." His coaxing, soft request played havoc on her vulnerable heart.

After what seemed like an eternity to him, Sarah answered. She was determined to keep to the obvious and logical points. Her own growing feelings for him had to be pushed into the shadows. "The financial benefits are hard to refuse in my present circumstances. Even a marriage of convenience must be terminated by a divorce. That bothers me because I believe in 'forever after'."

Brent was surprised to realize that he, too, had believed in pledging his love to one woman for the rest of his life. For the first time he questioned what had happened to make him throw his beliefs away. Or was there a possibility that something wonderful could happen in the coming year? What if—But his thoughts were interrupted by Sarah.

"In addition, I'd have to live a life full of lies. I'm an honest person," she said.

She turned her palms out and up in a gesture of distress. "I can't give you an answer now. I have to think about it."

"Of course. I've been considering only myself. Forgive me." He had to add, "But I only have a short time left."

"This is Friday. I'll give you my answer on Monday. You'll still have time to find someone else if necessary."

Without looking back at him, Sarah quickly left the room.

Brent watched her leave, seeing the ill-fitting suit and wishing he could see her dressed as she deserved. He asked himself if he was deliberately fooling himself into believing a strictly platonic marriage was possible with such a lovely woman.

Once outside Brent's office, Sarah paused to calm her racing heart. Her thoughts whirled in dizzy circles. She couldn't believe what had just happened.

Brent Chambers had asked her to marry him.

She walked slowly to her computer station, her flat-heeled shoes slapping lightly on the tile floor. She glanced at her suit coat draped over the back of her chair. Too bad she hadn't worn her new spring outfit today. When she entered Brent Chambers's office instead of personnel, she knew she must have looked totally drab. Yet he had asked her to marry him—was it because she looked the part of a person who needed what he had to offer? The thought of his pity made her writhe with pain. She pushed the thought away.

Debbie Sinclair turned to her. "Did you get your raise?" They'd worked side by side in the huge, noisy office as computer clerks since Sarah came to Chambers Arts and Crafts Company.

"No. Mr. Chambers—"

"Hey, you met with Mr. Chambers?"

"Yes. He told me there will not be any raises for at least three months."

Though Brent hadn't asked her to keep the proposal confidential, she knew she must. Debbie would be told only about the refusal of the raise.

"What a bummer. You were counting on the extra bucks." Debbie left her chair and hugged Sarah. "You need a break. Let me treat you to lunch later." As an after-thought she said, "And you can tell me all about how it felt to be right up close to that hunk!"

Debbie gave a huge sigh, wiggled her eyebrows and sank out of sight behind the divider.

Sarah laughed. She could always count on Debbie to lift her spirits. When Debbie went to join her Navy husband in Florida in two weeks, Sarah was going to miss her so much.

Sarah watered her thriving African violet plant on the corner of her desk and changed the angle of the the picture of her beloved young nieces. Arnie, her brother, was one lucky guy. He had a loving wife and family. Too bad they lived in California and she rarely saw them.

She switched on her computer, but her fingers lay idle on the keys and she stared at the blank monitor. She recalled the interview.

Brent Chambers.

Today, when she had stared defiantly at him, she had seen the tiny laugh lines at the corners of his eyes and mouth. She wished he had smiled his mega-watt smile at her.

She resented her response to his innate charm. She had vowed never to care for a man again, to love again. Life had proven uncertain, and permanent happiness, an illusion. After only six months of a warm and loving marriage, Johnny had died and left her alone and devastated.

As though it was only this morning, she recalled the phone call and heard the doctor from Memorial Hospital say, "I'm sorry, but your husband expired in his sleep at six this morning."

His heart had stopped with no warning.

The disbelief and the pain in her heart at the terrible news was as sharp this moment as it had been two years ago. Tears threatened to fall, but she blinked them away. Friends had assured her that time would heal. In a way, it did but, like today, she still was capable of experiencing all the sorrow and anguish of that horrible morning as sharply as ever—

Oh, Johnny, why did you have to die and leave me?

He had loved her with all his heart and always made her feel special.

Would another man do this in the new life she was forging for herself? She could only hope.

That evening, Sarah went home to her small apartment with her thoughts and feelings in turmoil. Romantic fantasies fought with the mundane consideration of Brent Chambers' offer.

Instead of one year, would they fall in love and live

happily ever after? Ah, to find safe haven in the solid warmth of a man's arms and enjoy the pleasures of marital bliss—in luxury and wealth.

She should accept his appealing offer.

Then, again, what did she know about this man? His physical attributes were enough to make a woman swoon. His business practices appeared to be above reproach. A fair and considerate employer, he gave his employees free medical and dental insurance and other benefits.

However, he could just as easily turn into a disagreeable man in the privacy of his home instead of an honorable business partner in this marriage of convenience. She would like to believe the latter was the case, but—

No, she should reject his offer.

Accept—reject—whirled in her head and made the weekend a nightmare.

By Sunday night, she took control of the tempest in her head. After sharpening her pencil, she pulled a lined pad toward her. She lettered FOR and drew a line down the center of the page and AGAINST on the other side. She'd get everything down in black and white and make an intelligent decision about her life.

The items on the FOR side were few, but they were heavy in financial weight. The monthly payments were hers for a year even if the marriage ended sooner. She'd be able to take day courses and finish her college degree at the end of this year of marriage. And still have money in her bank account.

The promised alimony payments weren't on the list. She had no intention of taking advantage of that clause in the contract. Once the marriage ended, she wanted no further contact with Brent. It would be too distressing.

Brent.

When had Mr. Chambers, her boss and owner of the company for whom she was a lowly computer clerk, become *Brent*? It must have happened when he started calling her Sarah instead of Miss Gordan. How easily the transition had occurred.

AGAINST.

To the world this was to be a real marriage. A very real, legal marriage which could only be terminated with a very real, legal divorce. Marriage vows to love and honor were until death-do-us-part.

Vows she'd already taken.

Sarah blinked away the tears. She knew she'd never forget the happiness of her first love. But Johnny would want her to add another love to her life. He'd want her to go on.

But how could she go against her moral belief and take the marriage vows when she lied?

She would have to live in the same house with a man who was a stranger to her. They hadn't even gone out to dinner with each other! What habits did he have? Her mother believed you had to live with a man to find out what he was truly like underneath the façade. This went two ways. What if they weren't compatible? It could easily be a hellish year. What if he turned out to be mentally and verbally abusive? She refused to even contemplate he would ever physically hurt a woman, but . . .

She'd have to lie to her parents and her brother that she was in love. She couldn't tell them the truth. They'd never approve. Love was the only basis for marriage.

Yet, a year wasn't that long, and look at the long-range benefits. The money and the opportunity to live in luxury whispered to her to put her conscience on the back burner, seducing her moral principles.

Sarah groaned and put her head in her hands. Too many lies. The money and the promised luxury weren't worth it. Yet, it was so easy to imagine life with no money problems at all. She could be good the *rest* of her long life—just this one year—how it beckoned to her!

She should stop fooling herself with her list of logical reasons to refuse Brent. Her gnawing worry was she'd lose her heart to him and he'd break it into tiny pieces! That, and that alone, was the real reason she was going to refuse his proposal of a loveless marriage.

Sarah straightened her back and put up her chin.

Monday she would reject Brent's offer.

If she lost her job, she'd find another one. Hadn't she done it before? Let Brent solve his own problems.

She flipped on the TV to a news station. She had no interest in what was happening in Paris, especially about a wedding between two Americans. Ready to change channels, hearing the names made her gasp and turn up the sound.

The newscaster was saying, "The wedding between multi-millionaire Thornton Bixley and Ashley Kirkland, a little known socialite from a small American city, took everyone by surprise. Since he was the eligible bachelor of the season, this was a real coup for the lovely American. They plan to honeymoon in Monaco."

For her wedding, Ashley wore an elegant white dress with a heavy gold belt. Diamond and gold bracelets circled her right wrist and large, diamond-studded gold hoops in her ears swung back and forth. She was a breath-taking picture in white and gold.

Sarah recalled her black and gold outfit the day she came to the office. Ashley apparently was obsessed with gold—with diamonds thrown in today. A gift from the wealthy groom?

She looked at the bridegroom and gave a gasp of disbelief. Thornton Bixley was shorter by inches than Ashley and had a definite pouch and a bald head.

She left handsome, wonderful Brent for that man? Had it been for love? Remembering Ashley's cold demeanor when she came to see Brent, Sarah doubted it. Thornton's money and social position seemed a more probable reason.

Money. The world revolved around it. She shouldn't criticize Ashley for wanting it. Hadn't she contemplated selling her soul for it, too? Johnny and she married for love. If she ever married again, it would also be for love.

Having made her decision, Sarah tried not to think of Brent. After all, he only wanted her so he could get money, too. Not a noble cause at all. Still, it was hard to find any comfort in her decision, to give up her one chance to live in the same house and see him every day for a whole year.

Chapter Two

As she walked from the bus to the door of the office building, Sarah smiled. On this sunny spring Monday morning the golden daffodils were out in all their glory in the park across the street.

"Thank heavens you finally got here," Brent's imperious voice pulled her up short.

"Wh—what's wrong?"

Brent had waited for her before the entrance to the building. Putting a hand under her elbow, he guided her out of the stream of people entering.

"Please, come with me into the park to talk."

They sat down on a bench. Brent didn't wait. "I hope you're going to say yes. I need you to do so more than ever."

"What happened? Did the stock market crash or something?"

"My accountant called me early this morning with the worst news. When you left on Friday, I had decided I would forget about my inheritance and get along as best I could without it. But now, I can't. Without the money, I'll have to file for bankruptcy."

"Oh, no. Will you have to close down, throw every-one out of a job?"

"Yes. And all the years I've put into the company would be thrown away."

Brent's voice sounded so bitter and bleak Sarah wanted to put her arms around him and comfort him.

"What about a bank loan?"

"It would be like putting a bandaid on a ruptured heart. What a mess I've gotten myself into—all because I didn't think through the future ramification of my expansion program. I never should have started building my megastore in the mall. The national economy was shaky and, like a fool, I didn't listen to the experts. I thought I knew better than they. Now, I'm paying the price."

"I'm so sorry, but I can't help you." Sarah looked away from his stricken gaze. "After thinking about your offer all weekend, I can't accept. I'd have to give up my principles. The money and the luxury of living in your home isn't worth my peace of mind." Sarah encouraged him, "You still have time to find someone else."

"Please. You're the only one. I've never begged a woman before for anything, but I'm begging you to-day."

Beg? How desperate must Brent be to humble him-self, for the first time in his life to beg—

"I can't." Sarah heard how weak her answer sounded. She wanted to help Brent. A year—that was all. And a lot of good could come from it. Besides, such an opportunity came only once in a lifetime. She'd be a fool to pass it up. Surely she could live with her conscience for such a short time.

Sensing her hesitation, he tried one more time, "If you want more money—"

"Your contract is fair and generous. But living a lie—pretending, day after day—it's so complicated!"

"I see." Brent dropped his head in his hands in defeat. He had no arguments with which to sway her. In fact, he felt guilty for asking Sarah to lie. Also, wasn't he feeling guilty about not fulfilling the terms of the will honestly? It was a no-win situation. He'd have to let events take their course and start all over again. He lifted up his head and turned to Sarah.

"I won't bother you again. It probably wouldn't have worked anyway." He stood up. "Come, time to go to work."

She blinked back the tears which filled her eyes. She ducked her head to hide them from Brent. To refuse him broke her heart. He didn't deserve to have his world tumble down around him. But he still had time until the May fifteenth deadline. Once he got back to the office, he could start a new search. The thought of another woman being his wife stabbed Sarah with unexpected pain. She suppressed it instantly. No one was going to be his true wife, not this year anyway.

They didn't talk as they rode up the elevator.

"Goodbye, Sarah," he said as he stepped out. He quickly strode toward his office.

Sarah's steps dragged on her way to her computer station, all the beauty of the morning gone. When she saw Debbie hadn't come to work, she was thankful. She didn't want to talk to anyone.

All day, while she did her routine work, she struggled with her thoughts. Her gaze went often to Brent's door. Had she made the mistake of her life? Why couldn't she just change her attitude? Why be so rigid?

Why not help Brent and help herself as well? Why not believe in her fantasy of Brent falling in love with her?

Doggedly, she did her work. And then worked on her own proposal to him. After he read it, he could refuse her and she'd be off the hook.

At five o'clock, she marched to the reception area before Brent's door.

"Please, I have to see Mr. Chambers."

Seeing the pale face and the pleading brown eyes, the receptionist nodded.

She tapped on the door and opened it at Brent's command. "I'm sorry, sir. Miss Gordan insists on seeing you."

"That's all right. I'll see her. You can leave for the day. Good night."

Sarah gave Brent a hesitant smile.

"Please, sit down." Brent longed to blurt out the all-important question. But he wasn't going to beg again. It would be too humiliating. He pursed his lips and sat down behind his desk. Adjusting the band on his wrist watch, he swept the papers on his desk into a crooked pile. Not trusting himself to speak, he raised his left eyebrow in a silent question.

The corners of Sarah's mouth trembled upward slightly. The words rushed out, "I've changed my mind. I'm willing to become your wife in-name-only for a year."

Brent smiled broadly. He left his chair and came to stand before Sarah. Impulsively he took her hands in his and placed a kiss on the back of each one, his breath warm against her skin. His romantic gesture surprised Sarah, as did the way her heart hammered in her chest and her lungs hungered for oxygen. She admonished herself it was just a show of his gratitude, for heavens sake, and nothing more. Her response to his handsomeness was what she had struggled with during the day. It had forced her to draw up her own terms.

She pulled her hands away.

"Your gratitude may be out of order. You haven't heard me out."

Brent leaned against the desk, his feeling of relief taking a nosedive. For a man who always controlled situations, this woman was doing a good job of making him feel incompetent, and he didn't like it one bit. But she *did* have the upper hand, for now. His gaze dropped to the folded sheets of paper in her hands.

"You gave me your contract, with your offer." She paused. She disliked the mercenary—even greedy— sound of her first demand. However, he said this was a business agreement. She was a businesswoman and she wanted a part in the negotiations. How much money she received was one issue she could have a say in.

"Here are my additions to your contract. You didn't offer me the physical protection I want."

Brent read her demands aloud, ". . . in addition to financial benefits, you will pay all my tuition and college costs until I get my degree."

Brent sucked in his breath. Not at the cost of her demands, but because Sarah was playing hardball. She wasn't going to meekly agree to his every wish. He read on, ". . . want to be protected from mental and physical abuse while I'm your wife. If it occurs, I won't be obligated to keep our arrangement confidential as I seek redress from our judicial system."

"What?!" exclaimed Brent. His good character had

never been brought into question before today. He glared at her.

Sarah smiled. "You know a woman must be careful these days. We will be together for a long time, tempers are sure to wear thin at times."

The year hadn't even started and already she was pushing his buttons. His temper wear thin? Like now?

What was he getting into? He'd thought this was going to be a simple cut-and-dried agreement. However, he was against the wall and had to accept her conditions. He admitted she had a valid point. She won his grudging admiration for wanting to get the best deal and to protect herself. He hadn't thought how daunting it would be for a woman to move into the house of a strange man.

"Anything else bothering you? Let's get it out."

"I don't know if I can fit into your social life and entertain your friends and colleagues as a wife should." Sarah held her head high and looked into his eyes. She had lived in a middle class society and even struggled with poverty at times. Oh, she knew which fork to use, but she had never traveled or talked with sophisticated, blasé men and women before. She could see how unacceptable she would appear to them as an employee of his. Had Brent thought of this?

"Not to worry. My uncle and I never entertained at home. We went to restaurants when we needed to do so. There's no reason to change this arrangement."

Sarah looked at Brent and shook her head. Brent didn't understand social pressure and how different his status would be once he married. She'd worry about it later.

"If that's all," he said, "make yourself comfortable while I make new copies of our agreement."

At the copier, Brent gritted his teeth. He tried to ignore Sarah humming "Night and Day" as she wandered around the office looking at the pictures on the wall. Her elusive fragrance invaded his senses. It made him think of wild flowers and sunny meadows, the lazy hum of bees and the lilting songs of birds. And picnicking in the daisy-littered grass.

He swore under his breath. How could he be thinking of romance and flowers even as he typed her demand for physical protection from him! He must be going mad. The first doubts of the success of his scheme rang bells in his head. He silenced them and concentrated on the contract. He pressed the print key.

"I hope this meets with your approval."

Another of her deceptively sweet smiles as Sarah read it through—twice. Her brows drew together thoughtfully as she checked a line again.

He wanted to shout, *Enough, enough of this torture!*

"Yes, I agree. I'll sign it."

"Good. Now to get down to business. We'll be married this coming Friday. That gives us five days of grace before the deadline. We'll need blood tests. Do you have a family doctor?"

Sarah nodded her head. "I'll do it as soon as I go home."

"I'll make arrangements with a Justice of the Peace to perform a civil ceremony—" Brent stopped. "Unless you want a church service?"

"No church service." Vows to love and honor, in a church, for this sham of a marriage? She pushed aside her sudden, vivid memories of another wedding, of walking down the aisle in her white gown and gossamer veil, of placing her hand in Johnny's loving one, and of vows of " 'til death do us part.' " A parting which death had wrought so cruelly.

Oh, Johnny, why did you have to die, her heart cried anew.

As though it was yesterday, the hurt and the pain were so sharp tears gathered in her eyes and threatened to spill down her cheeks.

Sarah got up abruptly and walked to the window, blinking her eyes to keep from crying in front of Brent. It was good the memory had surfaced at this time. It hardened her determination never to fall in love again. Certainly never with her new "business partner." To him, marriage meant needed money, nothing more.

When she turned back to face him, Brent was bewildered at the cold look Sarah directed at him.

"We'll spend the weekend at the St. Royal Hotel in Arlingford. It's fifty miles away so we'll have our privacy. Is that all right with you?"

"Anything you say," Sarah answered in a monotone.

Her matter-of-fact acceptance irritated Brent. She should show some emotion. It wasn't every day a woman consented to marry. But, he recalled ruefully, this was only a marriage of convenience. Even so, he, for one, experienced an irrational feeling of anticipation. The future promised to be interesting, especially since an intriguing woman was going to live with him.

"Shall we confirm ten o'clock on Friday, May tenth?"

"How fortunate I said yes." Sarah said bitterly. "Evidently, you had this all planned before I even gave you my answer." She added, "Just remember, I'm to have my own rooms in your house. I'm not sharing a bedroom with you no matter what the will implies!"

"Don't worry. I don't want you there." But the lie caught in his throat.

Thank goodness Sarah had brought up the subject. He'd tell the servants to make her suite ready for her. He had the uncomfortable feeling they clung to the old-fashioned belief that a bride and groom should share the same bed! He did, too, come to think of it. But he had promised Sarah that there would be no marital intimacy and he'd have to honor his word. Put her in the bedroom next to his—a viable solution to the problem.

"Make arrangements for your clothes to be sent to my house on Friday morning. I'd like you to see where you're going to live—"

"No. I'll see the interior soon enough." A shiver ran down Sarah's spine. If she saw it before she said "I do," she might lose her courage.

"Since you have everything in order, I'll go home," she said. "Under the circumstances, I'll need to take the rest of the week off. See you at ten on Friday at City Hall."

Without looking back, Sarah left the room, leaving Brent with his mouth open and unable to give any more commands.

Chapter Three

At 10:30 on Friday, Brent paced the floor at City Hall. To the amusement of the clerks, he had been doing this for the past half hour.

He had spent a miserable four days. Sarah hadn't contacted him. His fears forced him to call her last night to make sure she'd be here today. She had cut off the call with a terse, "Yes."

Brent looked at the clock on the wall behind the counter and checked it against his wrist watch. She was late. He scowled.

Behind him he heard Sarah apologize, "Sorry I'm late. There was a traffic jam."

Brent turned, a ready, scathing retort on his lips. He gaped, in speechless surprise.

He had assumed Sarah would come dressed in her office attire. As an afterthought, he had bought a corsage of small pink roses for appearance sake. He wished now he had ordered an old-fashioned bouquet of lilacs, tulips and roses, surrounded by a collar of ruffled lace like the one he recalled seeing on a Victorian valentine.

To Sarah, a wedding—whatever the kind—was a big occasion. Even though this one would take place in a dreary, dusty room in City Hall, with no romantic frills, Sarah determined to make it an unforgettable event in Brent Chambers' life. She would be dressed like a bride, one a man would be happy to marry.

To Brent, Sarah was a vision in a pale blue suit with small seed pearls on the lapels of the jacket. On her head was a straw hat with a froth of blue tulle cascading down her back. Her glasses were gone and her eyes, shadowed expertly, looked enormous and mysterious. Her lightly rouged lips were full and intoxicating.

"What a lovely corsage, darling. Please pin it on me."

In a daze, Brent did as she asked, never feeling the prick of the pin in his finger.

Of the signing of the forms and the brief marriage ceremony, Brent later remembered only snatches of phrases. "In sickness and in health . . . for richer or poorer . . .'til death do us part. With this ring, I do thee wed . . ." He had slipped the plain gold wedding band on Sarah's finger with a hand that trembled. Then came the irretrievable words, "I now pronounce you husband and wife."

"You may kiss your bride," instructed the beaming Justice of the Peace.

Sarah lifted up her face to him. "Oh, darling." Her loving term of affection, breathless and low, intimated deep feelings of joy to the witnesses.

Brent meant the kiss to be a chaste touching of cool lips. But Sarah's lips were so soft he was lost in the pleasure of the moment. His blood boiled in his veins and his heart thundered in his chest.

Sarah pulled away with effort. Heat spiralled within her. The kiss was wonderful.

Remembering the true nature of the wedding, she slid her lips to his ear and whispered, "I've brought Mr. Richards to be our photographer. We may need pictures to show to your lawyer. Besides, I want some pictures for my family."

Brent came down to rude reality. Sarah, in spite of her fabulous wedding outfit and disturbing kiss, hadn't forgotten this wedding was a farce. Even though he admired her single-mindedness, his male ego was bruised. He should have hired the photographer. And, yes, he wanted a picture of Sarah for himself. His beautiful bride.

Mr. Richards knew his job.

"First, a traditional shot of the happy newlyweds. Face each other and gaze into the eyes. No, no, come on, show your feelings for each other. Don't be so stiff. Good. Kiss your bride, Brent. Good . . . another one. That's a wrap-up."

Brent's self-confidence was shaken and his prosaic world turned upside down. The photographer's requests had stretched his self-control to the limit. Gazing into Sarah's soft, appealing eyes and kissing her again made him realize a startling fact: this was a preview of a year of pretending to love each other. The magnitude of the task unnerved him, but it was too late to back out of their agreement. He had to remain strong and businesslike.

Brent led a smiling Sarah to the waiting limousine. It smoothly left the curb, speeding them to their honeymoon weekend.

He sat stiffly beside her. "You look beautiful today, Sarah. I . . . er . . . didn't expect—" He looked at her more closely and demanded, "Where are your glasses?"

"I don't need them." Sarah grinned at him. "They're plain glass and I wear them to look more business-like." This was no time to tell him the glasses helped to avoid unwanted attention from obnoxious males.

Silently cursing this marriage of convenience of his own making, he wished Sarah would snuggle up to him. He felt punch drunk. Sarah, in her bridal outfit with her sweet kisses, had thrown him off in a big way. Worse, he was sure she had no idea how dis-turbing those kisses for the Justice of the Peace and the camera were for him.

When they entered the lobby of the St. Royal Hotel a short time later, the patrons looked with interest at the radiant bride and the proud groom. For them, Sarah hung on Brent's arm and gazed lovingly into his eyes.

Perhaps Sarah had missed her calling, thought Brent resentfully, and should have become an actress. She was a darn good one, today.

Brent had reserved the bridal suite. Bouquets graced the tables and a bottle of champagne chilled in a silver bucket.

Sarah walked across the wide expanse of deep car-pet to the bedroom door. Here, too, were bouquets of flowers. A white lace bedspread covered the king-size bed with dozens of satin pillows against the quilted headboard.

Brent followed Sarah and stared over her shoulder at the bed. He groaned silently. He wouldn't be sleep-ing there. Not with the irresistible woman who was now his wife . . .

Sarah strolled back into the living room and inspected the couch. She looked at Brent from head-to-foot and giggled.

"It's a little short, but you'll have to make do—or, the rug looks soft—"

"Never mind. I'll manage." Brent was more than a little put out. Nothing today had gone as expected. Where was the pliable woman he had dreamed of marrying? And would he be able to control his emotions for this unusual woman?

He had had little sleep all week and longed for a good night's rest. When he reserved the bridal suite, he gave no thought of the bed situation. Hadn't he wanted this marriage to be accepted as real? Of course, the honeymoon would take place in a plush bridal suite. Of course, there would be only one bed. Sarah, however, didn't need to laugh at him.

With a toss of her head, Sarah chuckled again and sat down. Her hat landed on a side table. She unfastened the straps on her sandals and kicked them off. Stretching her legs and wiggling her toes, she said, "Oooh, that feels good. These new sandals pinch my feet. Hope you don't mind."

Brent tore his gaze away from her shapely legs. He wondered if she knew how graceful her movement had been.

"I think it went well, don't you?" she asked with her eyes wide. Innocent concern furrowed her brow. "I'm sorry if I made you uncomfortable, but those adoring looks were necessary. Don't worry, they were only for the witnesses and the camera."

Ignoring his scowl, she continued, "How nice of the hotel to give us some champagne. Let's open it so we can toast our new life as husband and wife."

Brent ground his teeth at her mocking words. Silently, he opened the bottle. When Sarah jumped at the pop, he smiled at her, his good nature restored. He poured the drinks and they touched glasses.

"To our success," toasted Sarah.

"To our happiness," Brent answered, to his surprise. When had the saving of his company taken a second place in his list of priorities?

Sarah nodded in agreement. They needed both toasts to take them through this impossible venture.

"What are we going to do with ourselves until Sunday?" Sarah asked. She wanted to keep busy so she wouldn't have time to think—think about the way she had rationalized her principles away for reasons no longer black or white. Her desire for security, her dreams of a happy, second marriage, her intense and disturbing feelings for the man who was now her husband—all these ran together and she no longer knew which one was dominant.

"First, we'll have lunch," Brent suggested. "Shall we see what the hotel dining room has to offer?"

"Give me fifteen minutes to change." She hoped he'd be proud of her. She had spent all her savings on new clothes.

Sarah was back with a minute to spare. She wore a simple dark green sheath dress with a short jacket over it. The green complimented her shiny brown hair. It tumbled around her shoulders in a soft cloud. Brent wondered how it would feel if he ran his hands through it. If he only dared . . .

He struggled to adjust to the changes in the appearance of his in-name-only wife. Where was the drab little mouse who had asked for her deserved raise a mere week ago? When she had shed the ill-fitting clothes, she had, apparently, acquired self-confidence and poise. She was a woman to be treated with respect. He sensed life with her wasn't going to be dull. He suspected he'd seldom know what she would do next.

After lunch, they obtained brochures of interesting places to see in Arlingford. It had been the site of several Revolutionary War skirmishes and had two museums. The desk clerk also recommended they visit the boutiques and gift stores on the main street.

They strolled slowly, window shopping. Brent had never done this in his life. He found it intriguing to watch the emotions which flitted over Sarah's face when she saw something she liked. The urge to buy every item for her was strong.

"Do you like to dance, Sarah?"

"Yes, but I haven't for a long time."

"We'll go dancing tonight."

"But I haven't brought a suitable dress—"

Brent laughed easily. "We'll get one now."

He ignored Sarah's protests and steered her into a boutique whose show windows held only one manniquin and no visible price tags.

Though she had a weakness for beautiful clothes, Sarah resented his high-handed manner of gently directing her into the shop. And she was uncomfortable with the exclusiveness of the shop, a shop she'd never enter because the clothes were so expensive.

"Brent," Sarah said in a hissing whisper, "Stop it. I don't want you to buy me a dress here."

"Hush. Let it be a husband's gift to his new wife. Besides, we're on our honeymoon."

"I suppose, but don't get carried away with this husband thing. We're only business partners."

Brent looked into brown eyes brilliant with determination. Who was this bit of a woman, digging in her heels and reminding him of the rules? Why had he thought it was going to be easy? But he enjoyed a challenge, didn't he?

"Of course, my dear." Then he mildly said, "Shall we have the saleslady show you some dresses now?" On this score, he'd have his way.

They looked at several gowns before deciding on a classic dark blue cocktail dress.

"Darling, I love the gown. You're too good to me."

Brent smiled down into her eyes. He lowered his head and he whispered, "I think I see someone I know." It wasn't true, but he had to have an excuse to do what he had longed to do all afternoon. His lips covered hers in a long kiss, to kiss her again before he drew away.

"We were just married this morning," he explained to the saleslady who had been watching them with unabashed interest.

"Then you may want to look at some lingerie that has come in from Paris this morning," she urged.

Sarah gasped and felt the hot flush creeping over her cheeks. "Oh, no!"

Brent sat down and lounged on the fragile white and gold chair. "By all means, bring them out."

Sarah sank into her chair, knowing her husband had won this battle of wills. Well, that was the intent, wasn't it? Make it look real?

Sarah, oh'd and ah'd and blushed deeply at the choices made by Brent. Beneath her smiles and gay acceptance, she knew he'd never see her in any of them. Besides, he had made the rules for this year together. In private they were to be business associates and nothing more.

When they returned to the hotel, Brent dropped the packages on the bed.

"Are you going to model our purchases for me, my dear?" he teased.

Her answer was to point to the door and say, "Out."

With a laugh, Brent left, whistling a song with a catchy, happy tune.

Sarah shoved the lovely lingerie into the drawer of the dresser and slammed the drawer shut.

Dinner was by candlelight at a table overlooking the gardens, awash with moonlight and diamond bursts from far-off stars in a deep blue sky. They toasted each other with more champagne. When they danced cheek to cheek, their bodies joined in a single line with his hard muscles molding her soft ones. And acted, for all the world to see, like lovesick newlyweds with eyes only for each other.

Tonight, her feelings didn't know what was reality or what was fantasy!

And this was only the first evening of a year-long contract. She suppressed a groan of despair. How in the world was she going to hide the effect he had on her? Why, in her fantasy of a second perfect married life, had she given her Prince Charming the features of Brent? She did have Brent Chambers—but only as a partner-in-crime and not as a true husband.

"Brent," she urged, "Let's go upstairs—"

"I thought you'd never ask," Brent said with a wicked grin. "After all, I'm an impatient bridegroom."

Sarah ignored Brent's surly manner the next morning. She could understand having a kink in his neck and a miserable night was just cause to be a sorehead. Before the waiter delivered their breakfast, Sarah had quickly picked up the blanket and pillow from the couch. She felt sorry for Brent, but not enough to offer him a place in her bed. She tangled the covers and punched in the pillows on both sides of the kingsize bed. It looked as though they had—well, let the maid think what she liked!

After a shower, a shave and a hearty breakfast, Brent was ready to join Sarah to go sightseeing at the battle fields.

Later, they lunched at the Colonial Inn and went to both museums. By three o'clock Sarah saw Brent's lagging footsteps. They returned to the suite.

"You poor dear," she said, "You're all tired out. You can take a good nap before dinner."

"A good nap on that couch? No, thank you."

"Come on, I'll let you sleep on the bed." She hurried to add, "By yourself, of course. I want to read this history book."

"Sounds good to me." Although, he thought, it would be better if Sarah joined him. What a fool he had been when he blithely laid down the terms of this marriage. And Sarah wasn't making it easy for him to be strong and cold.

After Brent retreated into the bedroom and closed the door, an irrational desire to be with her husband, as in the past, almost made Sarah fling open the door and join him. Instead, she curled up on the couch and opened the book purchased at the museum.

Later, the bedroom door opened. Brent came into the room, yawning and running his hand through his hair. The corporate Mr. Chambers was gone and a sleepy-eyed man stood before her, smiling and happy.

Sarah's heart did a complete flip-flop at the sight. This man was her husband—if only!

"I needed the rest. Thanks for the use of the bed."

Sarah nodded, hoping he didn't see how breathless he had made her.

"Want to extend the invitation to tonight?"

"Don't push your luck, Mr. Chambers."

"Do you want to go dancing later?"

"Not really," Sarah answered, knowing it was another lie. It had been heaven to be held in his arms. "My feet are tired from all that walking. Let's have dinner sent in."

"Good. Besides, newlyweds should stay in the bridal suite."

Sarah blushed a rosy hue.

Brent laughed and suppressed the urge to tease her further. He called room service. When he turned around, he saw Sarah holding out her left hand and looking closely at the plain wedding band.

"A man in your position should buy his wife a proper diamond engagement ring. I'll give it back to you at the end of the year."

A sudden urge to shake her and then kiss her came over Brent. "When I give jewelry to a woman, I don't expect to have it returned. Whatever you receive this year will be yours. Do you understand?"

"Yes, Brent." Since her tone was so humble, he wouldn't have been surprised if she had added, "My lord and master."

She was laughing at him! She'd probably return the jewelry anyway. Sarah just wasn't going to jump at his every command. He no longer was her employer with the power to order her to do his bidding.

No, he was a mere inexperienced husband without a clue how to deal with an independent wife with a mind of her own.

And all he knew about his wife's previous life were the limited facts he learned from perusing her personnel folder. He had asked for it after she consented to marry him. He felt uncomfortable about doing it, as though he was spying on her. He should have gotten detailed information about her life at the time he asked her to marry him. But he had been so worried about saving his company that he had rushed headlong into this marriage. Still, he was relieved to learn Sarah had an ordinary family and education—no lurid past. Tonight they'd get acquainted with each other. Share important facts that might be asked by curious friends. Tell the same story.

"We know very little about each other," he said. "Can we talk?"

Sarah settled herself into the corner of the couch and nodded her head. She had so many questions. She'd been feeling frustrated because she had leaped before she had truly considered the hole she'd be landing in. Perhaps if she learned more about Brent she could more easily pretend to be his wife. But also, she needed to remember him as a hard-headed, business tycoon so she didn't really fall in love!

"What do you want to know?" she asked.

"Tell me about your parents and your brother and about anything else you want. People will be asking questions."

"Dad retired from the post office in Brenton in March. Mother, also, from her day care job. My big brother Arnie lives in Stratford, California, with his wife Alexandria and two darling daughters, Terry and Sandy."

"Why did you move to Brighton?"

"Because I—" She had almost said, I got married.

"I wanted to enroll in Brighton University. I was also able to get work in your company."

Sarah thought it logical that Brent had looked at her folder before he interviewed her concerning her evaluation. She hadn't included on her employment application her previous marriage. At the time she applied two years ago, she was still mourning her loss deeply. To put it down in black and white, for others to ask questions, was more than she thought she could handle. Leaving it out of her record assured her more time to get over it. After she had learned to cope with her grief, she shrunk from going to personnel with the information. Why stir up past events? It would be awkward to explain it all to Brent tonight. Her first marriage had no bearing on this marriage of convenience. And the comparison between two marriages and husbands was more than she wanted to think about. When the time was right, she'd tell him.

Sarah said, "Your turn."

She didn't tell him he had been an unending source of conversation and speculation by his female employees. Facts of his engagement, gleaned from the newspapers, were embellished and drooled over. Ashley Kirkland's appearances in the office and her participation in numerous charity events were discussed. Everyone thought she was a fabulous dresser and a very beautiful woman. And that the two of them made a very handsome couple.

Brent's story was quickly told: his parents' death and his life with his Uncle Matthew; private schools and then on to Harvard; joining his uncle in his firm until he decided to branch out for himself.

After reciting his life history, he realized his life had been truly dull. Yet, he had never felt unhappy or deprived in any way. He loved and admired his uncle and from his childhood wanted to be just like him. And he had patterned his life accordingly. Ashley had brought gaity and fun into his life during their all too brief engagement.

Brent fell silent. His thoughts filled with doubts about the coming year. What if Sarah became so bored with his quiet life-style she would leave him?

"Tell me about my new home situation and what will be expected of me when I walk through the door tomorrow."

Sarah hoped Brent wouldn't guess at how petrified she was suddenly feeling. Her home had been a modest ranch house in which her mother and she did the housework and cooking. Money had been budgeted carefully. But it was a happy home, filled with laughter and companionship. Homesickness stole over her. How she wanted to talk to her mother!

"There are four on my household staff—"

"Four—you mean you have *four* servants?"

"Well, yes. But you don't have to worry. They've been with me for years and are like family. They're pleased I've finally married. Do you want to hire your own maid?"

"Good heavens, no!" Dismay filled Sarah. She'd never be comfortable around four—yikes, four!—servants. She hadn't a clue how to deal with servants. A possible solution nudged aside her fears.

"I see no reason why they shouldn't continue just as they've been doing," she said. "It's no use upsetting your orderly home life anymore than is necessary."

Fat chance, thought Brent. He feared his orderly life was gone forever.

"What about your lawyer? When will you tell him about our marriage?"

Brent got up and walked to the window. Below him, people hurried along the sidewalks. Yellow taxis wove in and out recklessly. Uncomfortable, he turned back to her.

"Since I don't want to give Henry Stone the impression we married just in time to get under the deadline, I'll call him on Monday."

"Won't he think you married me on a rebound since Ashley left you to marry someone else? Ask if you've been in love with two women at the same time? That's how it would appear to me."

Brent paced up and down before the couch. Frustration caused a deep frown to furrow his brow. "I didn't think about this interpretation. What am I going to say, Sarah?"

"Of course, if we're really lucky, Mr. Stone won't question you. But don't bet on it. You can tell him relations between you and Ashley hadn't been close for some time before she eloped with another man. That's true, isn't it?"

Sarah waited for Brent's answer. She wanted to hear him say he wasn't broken-hearted by Ashley's action. When he told her about the breakup at the interview, she hadn't seen any great distress in his demeanor or in his voice. Since they were going to marry, there surely had been love and affection between them. He must be hiding his grief and heartache to be able to plan a marriage not based on love—love that had betrayed and humiliated him in the eyes of all the world.

Not saying the words she wanted to hear, Brent merely nodded his head. He remembered the occasions Ashley had been upset and annoyed with him for working so much. He hadn't taken her outbursts of temper seriously. For his blindness he had paid the price. This much of the story was true.

Sarah continued, "Because of the building of the megastore, everyone was putting in lots of overtime. You and I ended up working together. Being thrown together for many hours, we found ourselves falling in love. You were getting ready to break it off with Ashley, but she left of her own accord."

Brent smiled. "That sounds great to me. It could have happened just that way. But," he asked, "why did we get married so fast? Your family wasn't present."

"Have to blame it all on love. We couldn't bear to be apart a minute longer. And hope your lawyer had been in love himself at one time."

"He's a widower so he could be understanding."

Sarah felt uncomfortable about asking her next question, but she had to know, "If he asks about your feelings for Ashley, what will you say?"

Brent took his time before he answered. "I'll tell him the truth about how I still feel. Ashley and I have been friends all our lives and I'll always want to stay friends. But what I feel for you is different. It's been love from the beginning."

"Will our marriage be in the newspapers?" Sarah recalled her habit of checking the column.

Brent gave a groan. "Undoubtedly, but it's for the best. That way, we don't have to make any announcement and have fewer questions to answer." He thought a moment. "Perhaps Henry Stone will also see it. It'll make it easier for us."

"I'm sure the news will spread like wildfire in your office. We were always discussing such interesting items and speculating on them during our breaks and at lunch."

"What?" growled Brent. "I had no idea this went on."

"Sorry, but people do talk. After this weekend, they'll be trying to figure out how I managed to marry the boss! And right under their noses! But, in time, interest will die out as soon as something else happens."

Brent didn't look convinced. "I'll have to be more circumspect from now on."

"Don't let it worry you." She yawned. "Time for bed." She threw up her hands in mock regret. "Sorry, it's the couch for you. I'll get your blanket and pillow."

Brent watched the bedroom door close. Would Sarah wear the lingerie he picked out? He had to remind himself that this was a business relationship and was to last only a year. If love entered the picture, it was over. Next May, he would hunt in earnest for the love of his life with whom he'd live forever. Sarah had agreed to be with him for only a year. A year is not forever.

She was going to find it difficult to fit in with his business associates and sophisticated friends—especially Ashley, if she came back. They had nothing in common. He would help her during the coming year. She was doing him a great favor and he was grateful.

He sternly reminded himself that he had to avoid a romantic attachment by all means. At this point, a year felt like an eternity.

Chapter Four

On Sunday morning the taxi drove up the circular drive and stopped before the double oak doors with their etched glass panels.

This beautiful, gracious house was going to be her home for a year. It was huge!

As though on signal, a tall, white-haired man in a dark suit opened the doors.

"Symes, thank you," Brent said.

Brent smiled down at Sarah. He picked her up and carried her across the threshold. In his strong arms she felt like a fragile bird. She longed to have him cherish her and protect her from all heartache and unhappiness. He set her on her feet inside the door, but kept his arm around her waist. His physical support helped her to cope with her doubts and fears.

"Welcome to your new home, darling."

He pulled her closer to his side. Her eyes adjusted to the cool dimness of the entrance hall.

The floor was made of black and white marble squares. To the left, a graceful stairway with carved wood balustrades curved to the second floor. On the right, a table between two tall doors held a large bouquet of red roses.

Sarah tore her gaze from the flowers. With butterflies doing a jitter-bug dance in her stomach, she looked at the line of servants who faced her, undisguised interest in their eyes.

Last weekend, filled with curiosity, she had the taxi drive slowly past the red-brick Victorian mansion with the impressive scrollwork along the eaves. At that time she hadn't thought about the number of servants needed for an establishment of this size. Her heart beat furiously and the palms of her hands became moist. She clutched Brent's arm for support.

He looked down at her and smiled encouragingly. "This is my wife, Sarah."

He led her to the stout, maternal looking woman in a black dress with white collar and cuffs.

"This is Mrs. Ames, my housekeeper. Don't hesitate to ask her for anything."

Mrs. Ames grasped Sarah's hand and gave it a vigorous shake. She took over the introductions.

"Sadie's the best cook this side of the Atlantic. Mary's our maid and Symes will drive you anywhere you want to go."

Mrs. Ames beamed at Sarah. "You have no idea how happy we are Brent has finally gotten married, and to such a beautiful young lady. He didn't describe you as such."

Sarah lifted her eyebrows at this tidbit. What had Brent said she looked like? More important, did he remember to say he loved her? Surely the servants knew about the terms of the will. Of course, they were happy he had married. Their future was now secure. However, she couldn't dismiss their warm and sincere welcome. She began to feel at ease. She caught herself wondering whether they would have welcomed Ashley as warmly.

With the familiarity of an old family servant, Mrs. Ames ordered, "Brent, take your new wife up to her room so she can freshen up before we serve you the bridal luncheon Sadie prepared."

As she followed the other servants to the back of the hall, she said over her shoulder, "We did the best we could to make everything comfortable on such short notice. As you ordered, she has the bedroom and suite next to yours."

Sarah wondered if Mrs. Ames thought it was unusual the bride had her own bedroom or was this the acceptable arrangement in a large mansion as this one? If so, this boded well for their scheme.

Upstairs, Brent led Sarah to the second door on the right.

On entering, Sarah gave a delighted cry. "How charming! I love canopy beds."

When she walked around the room, her heels sank into the plush rose rug. The rose and blue colors were soothing to the eye.

In the comfortable sitting room the desk had a computer on it. Sarah gave a delighted smile of approval at seeing it.

"Thank you. It will be a big help to me. I always had to fight to use the ones at the college lab."

Brent felt as if he had been given the world. He had wanted to do something special for her and it was so good to know he had.

She added, "This suite is perfect. Mrs. Ames outdid herself."

Sarah opened the French doors leading to her small

balcony. Below were terraced gardens with riotous beds of spring flowers, a swimming pool and manicured, velvet-green lawns sloping gently to the edge of the Waddy River.

"Your home is lovely. I'll do everything I can to make sure you don't lose it."

He led her back through the suite to the door on the left wall of her bedroom. With slow deliberation, he put the key on her side of the door. She gave him a small smile. Not that she needed to lock him out. She knew her physical welfare was secure. While living in his house she was the one who would have to guard her emotions and her heart from him.

She walked into Brent's masculine, austere bedroom. A dark blue spread on the double bed showed a crease. Yielding to her housewife instincts, Sarah straightened the bedspread and, in passing, lightly caressed the pillow. She looked up to find his gaze following her actions.

Sarah blushed. She hoped he couldn't read her thoughts. For a moment, she had fantasized laying her head on the pillow beside his tonight!

She hurried through the connecting doorway into her bedroom. "I'll freshen up. Meet me in the hall."

The door slammed shut.

Brent looked at the door. It was sturdy and of thick oak. It didn't shudder, neither did it bang. He chuckled and began to whistle. Sarah was in his house and behind that door. For the first time in two days, he felt hopeful he would find happiness in the next year.

He walked to the bathroom sink and doused his head in cold water. Ye gads, and this was only the third day of their year together. Why had he brought such a provocative woman into his life and house?

He'd envisioned he'd marry an adoring wife, one who depended on him for protection and looked to him for guidance. A woman such as his old-fashioned uncle wanted for him. Sarah—she would never be such a wife. She was too independent.

Fifteen minutes later, Brent led the way to the dining room. Sarah gazed around with interest. Heavy red-velvet drapes framed the tall windows, with sheer white curtains billowing in the light May breeze. Polished, light-oak paneling covered the walls. A large oval table, with high-backed, crimson covered chairs occupied the center of the room. An intimate dinner for ten or twenty? Sarah trembled at the prospect.

Pictures of Brent's ancestors, in heavy gold frames, filled the walls. Were they looking askance at her for her temerity to marry into their highborn family?

Sarah resisted the childish impulse to stick out her tongue at them. Though this room and the rest of the house was daunting, she was here for a year—so there! She turned and smiled sweetly at Brent.

After seating her at his right, Brent leaned over and kissed her slowly. Delight surged through her and she leaned closer to him. She blushed at her response. Then she saw Mrs. Ames beaming at them.

How quickly she had forgotten this was a charade they were playing. It was going to be difficult under the constant watchful eyes of the interested staff. A silent groan seemed to rumble from the depths of her soul.

Brent was solicitous during lunch, anticipating her every want.

"Darling, have some more salad."

A minute later, "Here's some sugar—sweets for the

sweet," he said with teasing glee in his gaze. His fingers caressed the back of her hand.

She wanted to throw the sugar bowl at his head. Was he enjoying torturing her by his saccharine attentions? She had to get away from him.

"If you don't mind, I'm going upstairs and take a short nap—"

"Darling, a wonderful idea. I'll come, too."

Behind Mrs. Ames' back, Sarah scowled at him and mouthed, "No!"

Brent ignored her. His arm slipped around her waist and he propelled her toward the stairs. "A nap . . . we'll see."

Once upstairs, Brent dropped his arm and said briskly, "I'll go down to the study in an hour. You come downstairs when you want." He disappeared into his bedroom.

Sarah stared after him. A surge of disappointment threatened to swamp her. So what if he left her so abruptly? It was an act during lunch, wasn't it? She had to remember to be objective about their relationship.

A few minutes later, she soaked in the bubble-filled tub. If Brent touched her at every turn, being married in-name-only was going to be impossible. She'd talk to him and ask him to cool the caressing.

She changed into a comfortable pair of jeans and a loose yellow blouse with long, cuffed sleeves.

She felt prepared to face Brent in his study. At least there, with the door closed, they wouldn't have to show affection.

Brent welcomed Sarah's knock. Though he had tried to concentrate on his business reports, the events of the past week kept whirling in his head.

It had culminated with Sarah transforming herself into a beautiful woman. No wonder Mrs. Ames had been confused.

"Sarah's a short woman with brown hair. No great beauty like Ashley, but I love her."

It made his world tilt to one side to find out he was way off base in his description. She definitely wasn't like Ashley. She had a beauty all her own which fascinated him.

She shouldn't have touched his pillow, either. At lunch, the need to touch her to impress—well, no, he couldn't blame it on the servants. He longed to touch her for himself. He'd better cool things or he would drive her away. This was a farce, not a real marriage. An important fact to remember.

After she murmured her greeting, she said, "May I make a suggestion? Besides the engagement ring, a loving husband should remember the holidays and special anniversaries."

"I'll try to remember. If not, can I count on you to remind me?"

"Certainly." When she smiled at him, he saw again the elusive dimple in her left cheek play hide-and-seek. He resisted the urge to have his finger lightly touch her cheek and seek to catch it.

"Do we have time for a walk before dinner?" she asked. "I'd love to see the grounds."

Brent linked their elbows and laced their fingers together in easy comradeship. Once away from the house, she freed herself.

Conversation centered on the various plants and flowers. They reached the far corner where towering oak trees grew.

"Is that a tree house up there?"

His boyish grin transformed his stern face. "It sure is. Symes built it for me when I was ten. I wonder if the ladder is strong enough to still hold me. Let's see."

He tested each rung and climbed to the top, disappearing into the tree house. His head reappeared at the opening.

"Come on up. It's safe."

Sarah pushed aside her fear of heights. After all, this was a tree house, not a tall rocky cliff; a sturdy ladder, not a narrow rope.

Looking only in front of her, she began to climb. She expelled her breath. This wasn't so bad. She could do it. On the tenth rung, a squirrel scampered down the trunk. She looked down to follow his progress. A big mistake. She froze, her hands gripping the sides of the ladder. She felt stupid because she couldn't force herself to climb up the last two rungs.

Brent looked over the edge and saw the sheer terror in Sarah's eyes.

"Sarah," he cajoled, "look at me. Don't look down. Here's my hand. Grab it and I'll pull you up. Trust me." He wanted to add, "darling."

Sarah shut her eyes. With effort, she pried the death grip of her right hand. She stretched it up. When it was grasped by his strong hand, she gave a sob of relief. Her feet found the last two rungs and she tumbled into Brent's arms.

She clung to him. He raised her face and she thought he was going to kiss her. Instead, he scolded her. "Why didn't you tell me you were afraid of heights?"

Sarah pushed herself out of his arms and sat cross-slegged on the floor, her back against the sturdy timbers.

"I feel so stupid and foolish." Good thing he didn't know she foolishly wanted him to kiss her, not scold her. To get her mind off her fright and her disappointment at his reaction, she said, "Symes made this tree house. How long has the staff been with you? They seem like old friends and family."

"They were already here by the time I came to live with Uncle Matthew after the death of my parents. He did everything for me and the servants have mothered—and bullied—me ever since."

There was no indication from Brent's words he had been unhappy or lonely living with his uncle. To Sarah, his childhood lacked the elements which made up a family life—the companionship she had had with a protective, teasing brother and the love of two parents, especially a tender mother. She wondered if he felt the need for such a relationship in his life—a man and a woman loving each other and producing children. She wanted children. Did Brent?

Sarah reined in her errant thoughts and listened more closely to Brent.

"I hate not being honest with them about our relationship, but I'm also doing it for their good."

"I know it's hard for you. They'll be watching us because they're so happy for you."

"We better get back or Sadie's dinner will be spoiled."

Sarah gave a wail. "Oh, how am I going to get down?"

"No problem. You'll go down with my arms around you. You'll see. It'll be a piece of cake."

He wished their relationship was that simple. When he thought Sarah would lose her grip and fall, terror filled him. He wanted to hold her and never let her go.

But Sarah had quickly pulled out of his embrace before he made a fool of himself.

"Come, Sarah, down we go. Do as I say and you won't be afraid."

With his strong arms around her, the descent from the tree house was concluded safely. Sarah thought how long it had been since she had the comfort of a man's warm clasp about her.

"You'll never get me up there again unless you install an elevator."

"But you never looked at the fabulous view."

"View! I had all I wanted from the tenth rung of the ladder."

He laughed and gave her shoulder a squeeze.

After dinner they went into the living room to watch TV. On the surface, Sarah relaxed, laughing aloud at the sitcoms. She was very conscious of Brent and wished he was next to her on the couch. She wanted to snuggle up with him.

Brent covertly watched Sarah, wishing she hadn't chosen to sit so far away from him. They should be together, she was his bride, wasn't she?

Even though a wide space separated them, he was surprised to feel so much at home with her. As though they had always been together and spent their evenings with each other.

At 10:30 Sarah brought the evening to a close. "It's been a long day. I'm going upstairs."

"I'll lock up. Good night, Sarah. Thanks for everything."

Brent watched her leave. In his imagination he saw two bedrooms upstairs and a connecting door—a door which shouldn't separate a husband and wife. They were a couple only on a piece of paper, he sternly reminded himself.

As soon as she entered her bedroom, Sarah's gaze was drawn to the connecting door.

The die was cast. This was the first night in her new home. No matter how much she fantasized, Brent wasn't her true husband. This was business—made all the more difficult because they would have to show affection for each other. In addition, they had to keep the public demonstrations in the public realm only and never, never take them personally.

Though she had sorted out her thinking, Sarah still had trouble falling asleep.

Brent, being aware of Sarah only a few feet away, realized he was a husband whose wife was behind that closed door. And this situation was of his making, and would continue as he had contracted.

Coming down the stairs the next morning, Brent heard Sarah's laughter. He entered the dining room.

"Good morning, darling," she said with a warm smile.

Seeing Mary entering with the hot toast, he kissed her.

"Good morning, my love. I told you not to get up for breakfast this morning. You didn't get much sleep last night."

Sarah saw the maid beam and swore she could read her thoughts. Separate bedrooms? Not last night!

He watched the blush slowly spreading over her lovely face with fascination. When her fork fell from her trembling hand to her plate with a clatter, he gave a loud chuckle.

"You are my darling and always so thoughtful."

Sarah almost gagged on her own sugary words. What she was willing to do for their agreement.

After breakfast, she walked with him to the door, holding his hand. When he drew her into an embrace, she leaned her head against his shoulder.

"I'll come home early." He whispered, "Mary is watching."

"Goodbye, my dearest."

She waved until his car disappeared out of the driveway, bemused and confused at her reaction to what she was to regard as a stage kiss.

Suddenly, terror gave wings to her feet. She fled up the stairs and threw open the connecting door. She made her bed to pristine neatness. Brent's shirt and tie were flung to the foot of her bed.

In Brent's room, she tossed her sheer white chiffon and lace nightgown—a very bride-like gown—on the floor beside the bed. One dainty bed slipper was thrown near the window and the other at the foot of the bed. Both pillows were punched, and the sheet, tangled with the comforter, trailed to the floor.

One last frantic glance and she raced to her sitting room. She was leafing through a magazine seconds before Mary arrived to do up the bedrooms.

"There you are. I'll get out of your way."

Sarah did a little dance and sang, "Oh, what a beautiful morning, oh what a beautiful day!"

Mary gave an indulgent laugh. "It's good to see someone in love. Brent is a lucky man, Mrs. Chambers."

"Please call me Sarah."

"I think Mrs. Sarah would be more fitting."

"As you wish. I should go down and see Mrs. Ames."

When Sarah walked down the stairs, she felt as though a web was gradually being spun around her, a strand at a time. So many strands had already been spun—the contract, the wedding, calling each other darling, kissing, etc. Once started, telling lies became easier and easier. But it was only for a year. Then, she vowed to heaven, she'd never tell or think another lie the rest of her life.

Sarah assured the staff of servants they were to carry on as they had been doing. Sadie remarked, "We'll run the house. You just make our Brent happy."

Sarah fled out to the terrace, feeling her cheeks turning crimson. How she hated deceiving those kind souls. Although the birds were chirping and the fragrance from the flowers made the air sweet, she found it hard to appreciate her lovely surroundings.

And to think Brent and she had gone into this with "We're two intelligent adults. We can easily do it."

Yeah, sure . . .

She'd have all day to write letters to her parents, Arnie, and dear Debbie. If only she could talk to Debbie face to face. Too bad her husband became sick and she had to rush to his side last Monday. Debbie didn't even know she was married. When she read the letter, she'd scream!

Chapter Five

On Monday morning, Brent acknowledged his good luck with a grateful heart. Standing outside the elevator, his gaze roved over the outer office. No longer did he dread the beginning of a new day. His company was saved from ruin. The letter of the law had been observed, with five days to spare.

He squared his shoulders to receive the questions and expressions of congratulations for his marriage from the office staff and employees.

When Sarah told him they read the newspapers, she had been right. There was no need to make an announcement of an event already known to have happened. Though he did see the amazement in their eyes, revealing how surprised they were. There would be plenty of talk during the coffee breaks today!

But a much more weightier undertaking had to be considered. The call to Henry Stone. Hopefully he, too, had read the papers.

After exchanging greetings, Brent got to the point.

"Did you see Saturday's paper on marriage announcements?"

"To my great surprise. After seeing a CNN report of Ashley Kirkland's marriage to Thornton Bixley, I didn't think you would be able to meet the terms of the will." Henry Stone was silent, letting his suspicions get to Brent. "I hope you have a convincing story to tell me."

Brent's answer came out hesitantly, "Ashley and I hadn't been getting along for some time. She found life in Brighton dull and wanted me to go with her to Europe. I refused. My life is here and always will be. After she left, my feelings for a woman in my office proved stronger than I had realized." Brent gave a soft chuckle. "From the beginning, I was drawn to her and had watched her from afar. Since Ashley had left, nothing stood in my way to get closer and to declare my love."

Brent was surprised at the basic truth in his statements: he *had* felt like this for his little clerk. Could he translate this to Henry? He wasn't encouraged by the reply.

Henry Stone's voice sounded dry and suspicious. "I've heard of love occurring after only a short time, but I never believed it. Is this what you're telling me happened to you and—and this woman?"

"Sarah Victoria Gordan—Chambers—is her name. And, yes, it did." Brent suppressed the sudden longing to be truthful with Henry. Too much was at stake and he couldn't risk it. Their agreed story had to be told. "That's why I wanted to get married right away. Since her family couldn't come and I'm alone, we married simply. I hope you will wish us happiness."

The silence at the end of line lasted until Brent asked, "Are you still there?"

"Because of my past regard for you, I will accept

what you tell me and not stand in your way—at least for now."

"Please come to the house and meet Sarah. That's all I ask."

"I'll be happy to come." Henry actually sounded as though he was. "Come to my office at two this afternoon to sign the forms for the transfer of money to your account. Oh, yes, and bring your marriage license."

"Sarah, where are you?"

She hurried from the library thinking Brent sounded like a real husband coming home from work. A wave of longing swept over her for this to be true. Throwing her arms around his neck she meant the kiss to be a wifely peck. He, however, pulled her tightly against him and kissed her long and hard. Over his shoulder she saw Mrs. Ames. Sarah sighed with regret. Another act.

"Delay dinner for fifteen minutes, please. I've something to discuss with my wife."

Being called his wife gave Sarah pleasure—even if it was only for the benefit of their charade.

He steered her into the library and closed the door. Though he seated Sarah, he paced the floor before her.

"You were right about people reading the marriage announcements in the papers. Everyone in the office wished us happiness. I could see, however, that they were very curious about how it all happened. But at least that's over with. I called my lawyer. He'd read the papers also."

Brent stopped talking.

"Was he difficult? Is he going to contest your claim to the inheritance?"

"Though he had his reservations about whether people fall in love at practically first sight, he processed, at least for now, the will. The money is in my account and my company is again solvent."

"What a relief! What else?"

"Since he wanted to meet you, I invited him to dinner on Thursday. Is that okay with you?"

"Of course. By the time he goes home we'll make sure he believes we love each other and married only for that reason."

Brent wished he could be as confident as Sarah. But he did have faith in her determination to convince Henry.

"Let's go in to dinner," he said, "I'm starved. I didn't eat any lunch."

After the meal, Sarah asked, "Are you up for a walk? It's such a lovely evening."

Aware of the fond gaze of the servants, they strolled hand-in-hand down the winding paths of the garden. Sarah dropped her hold when they were out of sight of the house.

Brent was silent as though the events of the day had tired him.

The day had been long and lonely for her. Sarah was pleased just to have him with her. She was surprised that she should long to be near him so much. Was there magic in the words "I pronounce you husband and wife?" Had an invisible bond been forged between them, making them one? She did know something was happening over which she had no control.

The letters to her parents and brother had required much thought. She explained why they had married in such a hurry, implying a whirlwind courtship and the desire not to wait. She told them how wonderful her husband was and that he had been her boss. The body of her letters contained her detailed description of what she wore to the wedding and the interesting things they did on their brief honeymoon. And about the beautiful house and the servants who now waited on her, making a joke about her falling into a bed of roses. She assured them she would be financially secure. She hoped she was successful in convincing them she was very happy. She ended the letters with a vague statement about getting together when things settled down. She would also send wedding pictures later.

Debbie's letter contained the same information. However, since Debbie knew how few had been her encounters with Brent in the office, she had to weave a story of meetings and dinners after Debbie left for Florida. It wasn't hard to stress it was a whirlwind courtship leading to a quick marriage. She told her how much she missed her and promised to write often, to keep her up-to-date on everything.

No one was told it was a marriage of convenience with a one-year expiration date. She was surprised at her skill in writing so many words without being specific about the most important facts of her new life.

As soon as they sat down on the gaily striped seats of the white latticed gazebo at the bottom of the garden, Sarah spoke in a firm, business voice, "From now on, when we come down to breakfast, we'll have to leave the connecting door between our bedrooms open."

Brent raised his eyebrows. She had his full attention.

She continued and wished her heart would stop beating so fast. "I managed to run upstairs before

Mary came to do the rooms. After you made that remark at breakfast about me not getting much sleep—"

He burst out laughing. "That took you by surprise. Good thing Mary didn't see the murderous look you gave me."

To her consternation, she could feel a blush dyeing her cheeks. With difficulty she continued even though she felt her face getting pinker and pinker. Without looking him in the face, she told what she did in her bedroom. Then she went on to relate her next actions. "In your bedroom I arranged some more articles of clothing—"

"My, my, what articles and where?"

"I threw my bed slippers in two directions . . ."

Brent's eyebrow went up and a big smile appeared. He would have loved to see this.

"I rumpled up both of your pillows and tangled the sheets and covers . . ."

Brent laughed heartily. "Go on. I'm all ears."

"And, well, I—I—I dropped my nightgown on the floor by your bed."

The ardent speculation in his eyes made Sarah breathless.

He teased, "Was it a high-necked, cotton gown?"

"No, of course not. It was that sheer white chiffon and lace one you picked for me." She stifled a groan. She just knew, without a doubt, what Brent was hoping. *Would you model it for me tonight?*

She mumbled, "From now on, I'll knock on the door to let you know I'm going down to breakfast. I'll make my bed. Open the door before you go down— only make sure both sides of your bed look slept in."

"Are you going to drop one of your nightgowns?"

"No! Once is enough. The servants can use their own imaginations from now on!"

Oh dear, she thought, *was Brent's imagination working overtime?* Would the picture of them together remain in his thoughts? She knew it would be in hers. Before she betrayed herself, she changed the topic, "Did you say Mr. Stone is coming on Thursday?"

"Yes." Brent was grateful to have Sarah direct his thoughts to a safer path. And he marveled that Sarah could be so calm and businesslike. She evidently didn't suffer from romantic thoughts!

"The servants see what they want to see: you happy and in love with the woman of your choice," she said. "But Mr. Stone is already suspicious, and he has every right to be. We'll have to do some convincing acting."

"Shall I kiss you more often?" Brent asked hopefully.

"Heavens, no. Less is more and we won't be so apt to overact. Some hand-holding and shy kisses on the cheek. Speaking with our glances. Talk about the office and how I bumped into you and dumped all the files on the floor."

Brent recalled the day. When he looked deep into her expressive eyes, he had been shocked at the way his heartbeat quickened and his breathing became ragged. And he couldn't forget her. Watched for her to come out of the elevator and walk quietly in her rubber-soled flat shoes to her computer.

"Brent?"

He realized his thoughts had gone off on a tangent. "Mr. Stone will probably question you. Is that okay?"

"Of course. My life has been quite dull and ordinary. Going to work and to college classes. That's it."

Sarah dropped her gaze to her hands. She was troubled because she hadn't told him about her six-month marriage that day in the office. Or when they were exchanging their family histories the other night. She still shrank from talking about the sudden ending to her happiness. Didn't want to think it could happen again if she was fool enough to trust the fates and a special man with her happiness. To disclose it tonight would serve no purpose. It had no relevance to the present circumstances. It wasn't as if a man from her past would suddenly appear to destroy their well-conceived plan. But what if Mr. Stone decided to investigate her past? A huge fortune was at stake. The thought turned her heart to ice. He'd surely tell Brent—she wouldn't think about it now.

She bravely smiled at Brent. "Don't worry. We'll both do fine."

At the breakfast table the next morning, Brent said, "I'll have your credit cards in a few days. I already have charge accounts at Hardy's Department Store and H. C. Cline's. And use this for whatever else you want to buy."

Sarah's eyes widened at the thick wad of bills he placed on the table. She looked at him over the rim of her coffee cup, feeling uncomfortable about him giving her cash.

Guessing at her thoughts, he said, "Sarah, I want you to feel free to spend my money for your needs this year. Go shopping today and buy some clothes—a new dress for the dinner with Mr. Stone. Before an important dinner Ashley spent hours at Marcus Beauty Salon—"

Brent stopped. Sarah's lovely brown eyes were full of resentment and hurt. Had he just made a mistake

to order her to go shopping? She'd think he was criticizing her. And only a fool would bring an ex-fiancée
into the picture. "I'm sorry, I didn't mean—"

"I know exactly what you meant." Sarah rose from
her seat. "It's time you left for the office."

She walked with him to the door and raised her
cheek for his kiss.

"I'll call you," Brent said hoping to lighten the
strained feeling between them.

"Please don't. I'll be out shopping forever. There's
so much I need to buy so I can bring credit to you."
She didn't smile. "I can't wait to show you the new
me."

Brent knew when he was beaten. This husband business was full of pitfalls.

After Brent left, Sarah walked to the gazebo. Two
stray clouds scurried across the blue sky. The sun was
delightfully warm. The spicy fragrance of the white
and purple lilacs enveloped her. Swallows burst into
a wild song over her head.

She shut her eyes and ears to the beauty around her.
She wanted to wail and cry—to drown out the joyous
birds, to tear up the lilacs and trample on them. To
run away and never come back.

Brent's words this morning made it clear what he
thought of her clothes and her appearance. He didn't
have to tell her that she didn't fit into his world. That
she didn't compare favorably with the beautiful and
elegant Ashley.

Taking a deep breath, she straightened her back and
threw back her shoulders. No more self-pity. It wasn't
his fault. It was hers for dreaming of a possible Cin-
derella ending to this year. This was a business arrangement, a job. She would dress accordingly and get

herself transformed at her first stop, the renowned Marcus Salon.

The Sarah who left the salon had little resemblance to the one who entered. Her hair, cut in short layers, fitted her head like a sleek cap. A manicurist worked on her nails and a make-up artist accomplished wonders with eye makeup, blush and lip liner. She didn't think Brent would like the new Sarah look. She herself felt like a stranger and a fraud.

At the exclusive dress department at H. C. Cline's she found the perfect dress for Thursday. She bought three other outfits, vowing this was only the first of such shopping trips. Never again would Brent have the opportunity to order her to go shopping! Though she had never had much money to spend on clothes, she did know what was perfect for her. She'd be known as the best dressed young Mrs. Chambers.

She wore a bright red suit home with a seductive flair to the short skirt. It rounded out her new image.

In the yarn department she purchased yarn and instruction books. To help fill the hours, she would knit some booties and sweaters for her friend, Debbie. Her baby was due in January.

How she missed Debbie's friendship. She had no one to talk to, to share her fears and woes. The need to hide the true facts of her marriage had alienated her from her mother, her confidante all her life. Brent didn't know that she was a woman who was insecure and struggling with this farce of a marriage. She had never felt so alone in her life. More and more she was realizing how much it was costing her to continue. She would never let Brent see her vulnerable side. She'd always put on a brave front.

The money to buy all these lovely clothes was a

plus, but it meant nothing if Brent only compared her to Ashley—and found her lacking. One good thing, he was stuck with little old Sarah for a year and he'd better get used to seeing her as she was. At any rate, today's transformation did give her more confidence to meet his world.

When Mrs. Ames opened the front door, Sarah wasn't surprised at her reaction.

"Yes, it's me!" Sarah laughed. "Brent wanted me to go to the salon to make myself beautiful and do some shopping. I'm afraid I went a little overboard." She whirled around before her. "Do you like my new hair style?"

Mrs. Ames shook her head. "Mrs. Sarah, I liked the way you had your hair before. One good thing about hair, it'll grow again."

"How right you are. Please have Symes bring my packages to my bedroom. Thank you."

Sarah ran upstairs, feeling the woman's disapproving gaze burrowing into her back.

The connecting door gaped open, a mocking reminder of their duplicity. She longed to slam it shut and lock it, to be honest about their nightly activities!

Worrying about Sarah broke Brent's concentration all day. He hadn't wanted to hurt her by criticizing her clothes or her appearance. But ever since she entered his office wearing that hideous black, ill-fitting suit, he had longed to get her into the clothes that would do her justice.

Why had he foolishly suggested Sarah emulate Ashley's hours spent in making herself beautiful? He hoped Sarah wouldn't cut her hair. He liked to see it swirl about her shoulders with every toss of her head.

He'd like to see it grow even longer. He agreed with the old sages that a woman's crowning glory was her hair—the longer, the better.

Stepping into the house at the close of day, he wondered again what he would see.

"Sarah?"

"I'm in the living room, darling," she called.

Maybe everything was okay. His conjecture was premature. When he walked into the room, he sucked in his breath. Who was this stranger standing before him?

As if in a trance, he watched Sarah turn around slowly in a circle for his inspection, even giving a little swing to her hips. Her dangling gold earings gleamed in the light of the crystal chandelier.

"What did you do to your beautiful hair?"

"You told me to go to Marcus and they said this is the latest style." She gave her head a shake. "I like my hair this way. It makes me look more sophisticated, more like Mrs. Brent Chambers, don't you think?"

"No. I liked your hair longer."

"You should have said so this morning." She fluffed up the shiny cap. "Do you approve of my suit? It's a designer original."

"I don't like red on you. Don't wear it again."

Sarah's gaze seared him. "The salesperson thought it was made for me. And I shall wear it whenever I want."

The gauntlet had been thrown, figuratively, in his face.

"I only request you don't wear that suit on Thursday. Red has connotations—"

"Nonsense! Not in this day and age. But," Sarah

conceded, "I'll wear one of my other new dresses. Want to see the other things I bought? I did spend a lot of money today."

"I don't care how much you spent," Brent said through clenched teeth. "I'm going into the study until dinner is served."

Sarah sank into a chair and placed her head on the arm rest, tears rolling down her cheeks. Why had she been so hateful? But he *had* hurt her feelings this morning.

Too late, she realized Brent hadn't meant to hurt her. She had been too sensitive and insecure. But, since he came home, he had criticized everything about her clothes and appearance! He should have appreciated her efforts to follow his orders.

Never allowing herself to cry for more than a few minutes, she wiped away her tears and smoothed down the red skirt over her knees. How she had shocked him. Although he didn't like red, *she* did and she would wear it again if the occasion called for it. On this issue, she wouldn't be ordered about!

When Mrs. Ames came to announce dinner, Sarah tapped on the study door. Brent opened the door and saw the traces of tears. Remorse filled him. He reached over and his finger lightly touched her cheek. "I'm sorry. I've been an insensitive fool. Please forgive me?"

"No, it was I. Forgive me?"

"Done." His gaze traveled over her. "I—I'll get used to the new you." He walked around her and inspected the hair cut. "Well—it is very smart—I guess. It changes you—"

"No. I'm still the same. You'll see."

"Let's do justice to Sadie's dinner."

When they were alone in the living room afterwards, Sarah said, "I think Mr. Stone will talk to the servants about us. Servants observe the people they work for. When I worked as the upstairs maid for a rich family, the conversation in the kitchen was all about the family members and their activities."

"That job wasn't in your file."

"Unimportant. I only worked for two summer months." Sarah thought, another fact about my life I left out, but not to be compared in importance with my marriage.

Becoming conscious of Brent's scrutiny, she held up a partially finished blue bootie. "Isn't this cute? The booties are for my friend Debbie who worked beside me in your office. She's in Florida with her husband who's in the Navy. I've written to her and told her we were married. I can't wait to hear from her."

"Have you told your family?"

"Yes, I wrote a long letter to them."

When she didn't go into details, guilt made him uncomfortable. He had given no thought to her family and what she would tell them. He quickly made a decision. "If you want to tell them the truth about us, please do. Only I think it would be good if they kept our secret."

Sarah appreciated Brent's offer, but didn't feel she should act on it. "Thank you, but I'd rather not. I don't want them to be worried about me or spoil their visit with my brother. They're leaving next week. I'll invite them to visit us later in the year."

Fate had been kind to her to have her parents plan their trip before her wedding took place. Though they would always love and support her, she knew they wouldn't understand a marriage of convenience. It was from them she had acquired her repugnance of divorce except in extraordinary circumstances. To deliberately get married with the decision to divorce in a year would be beyond their understanding, nor would they condone it. It was best they never knew the truth—*ever*.

She tucked the bootie into her knitting bag. Had he and Ashley planned to have a family? Remembering Ashley, so slim and perfect in her gown designed by a top Paris couturier, Sarah couldn't visualize her "big with child." Then she felt ashamed of her spiteful thoughts. Of course any woman would be happy to have Brent's baby.

On Thursday night Sarah wore a dark green dress with a white Peter Pan collar. It made her look demure and without guile . . . just the appearance she wanted to make.

When they greeted their guest, Sarah had her arm through Brent's.

During dinner, Mr. Stone accepted seconds and praised Sadie's dinner. He appeared to enjoy the general conversation and frequently smiled at Sarah. She smiled back at him. She liked the man and appreciated his courtly manner toward her.

"Let's have coffee in the living room," Sarah suggested. She took Mr. Stone's arm and led him to the most comfortable chair.

She reached down to remove the magazine on the seat. A light blue ball of yarn rolled off with a partially finished bootie speared at the end of a knitting needle.

"Oh," apologized Sarah, "I forgot to take my knitting upstairs."

She picked it up and laid it on the side table.

Mr. Stone said nothing, but Sarah saw the knowing smile which pulled at the corners of his stern mouth.

Sarah hurried to explain. "My friend Debbie is having a baby in January and these are for her."

Sarah groaned silently. She hoped he believed her. Or was he thinking this was the reason for their quick marriage?

There wasn't anything she could say at this point. After time went by, he'd know the truth.

Mr. Stone took his time drinking his coffee. They talked about the fund-raising drive for the new library. He finally set his cup on the tray.

"My dear, I hope you will excuse me. I must have a few words with the staff about this splendid dinner. I'll be back shortly."

Sarah leaned back in her chair and sighed wearily. The evening had been a great strain. She initiated most of the conversation, but Brent had been quick to follow her lead.

"You've been wonderful tonight," he praised her. "No one would guess this is all an act."

Brent turned away from her. More and more, he didn't want it to be an act. He was enjoying being married to Sarah way too much. He no longer came home to an empty house. She made married life so easy and believable he was falling into the trap they were laying for others! If he wasn't so skeptical, he'd suspect he might be falling in love with his contract wife.

Sarah interrupted his disturbing thoughts.

"I'm afraid Mr. Stone didn't believe my knitting was for Debbie. It's natural for him to jump to the conclusion that that is the reason for our quick marriage." Sarah turned her head away from Brent to hide the flush of embarrassment—and spurt of longing. If it were only true! "At least, for now, he won't question us any more about our marrying just before the very end of the three-month grace period of the will."

Brent shrugged his shoulders nonchalantly. "Time will tell." Now he had another image to throw him a curve! The picture of a beautiful, pregnant Sarah telling him the wonderful news brought a smile to his face.

"I've had a very pleasant and enlightening evening," Henry said. "You two must let me take you out to dinner at my club in the near future. By the way, Brent, have you heard from your Aunt Hattie recently?"

Had Henry brought her up to make them realize that the other person in the will was a possibility? Sarah knew everything would have gone to his aunt if Brent hadn't married in time.

"I heard from her two weeks ago. She's well and keeping busy with her garden club." Brent didn't tell him he hadn't told his aunt about the wedding. He didn't want to answer her questions or have her rushing to visit him!

"Come see me tomorrow to sign some papers. These are interim documents and you won't receive your full inheritance and the title to this house for another year yet."

Brent looked into the bland face of the lawyer. Was he giving still another subtle intimation that they had a whole year to prove their marriage was legitimate?

"I understand. I'm not worried. I'm just thankful to have my operating money at this time. In a few months I'll have no need for any additional capital."

As soon as Mr. Stone drove away, Sarah excused herself. "I'm going to bed. It's been a long night."

"Go ahead. I've got some work I want to finish. I'll see you at breakfast."

Without further words, Brent left her at the foot of the stairs and escaped to his study.

At least "escaped" was the word Sarah used to describe his quick departure. He acted as though he couldn't stand being with her another moment. Was he feeling the strain of pretending? And they'd only been married a week. A long, long year loomed ahead.

Emotionally drained herself, Sarah's feet dragged on the stairs. Did Brent think she delighted in fooling a fine, upstanding man like Mr. Stone? After all, he was the one who had initiated this whole deception.

After entering her bedroom, she vented her frustration by slamming the connecting door closed and felt much better. She didn't care about the meaning of the action; she only knew it helped her feel better.

She pulled out a new nightgown which was one of six she had purchased on her shopping spree: a beautiful creation of white satin and lace.

She held it up to her cheek, loving the sensual feel of the satin.

The sound of the door closing next door made her jump. With her heart pounding and her face burning, she threw the nightgown away from her as if it were on fire.

She quickly put on the old, comfortable pair of blue pajamas. They were the only piece of clothing she had saved from going to the Salvation Army after Johnny's death. When she was feeling insecure and overwhelmed, she got comfort from wearing them, as though his loving arms were holding her close, protecting her from the world. Tonight, depression had begun to press down on her and she hated—*hated*—the role she played. And happiness seemed unattainable.

The pajamas were big enough to almost fit Brent. She hoped Mary would make such a connection when she found them in Sarah's pile of clothes to be laundered.

Sarah jumped into bed and pulled the sheet over her head.

After a night of broken sleep, Brent welcomed the buzzing of his alarm clock. He dressed and waited impatiently for Sarah's knock. She was late—unusual for her. He walked over to the door and put his ear to it. Only deep silence. He tried the door knob; it turned freely in his hand and the door swung open.

Walking softly, he went to the bedside of his sleeping wife. Her vulnerable beauty took his breath away. Her long lashes lay against the silky skin of her cheeks. He smiled at the long-sleeved pajama top she wore.

A man's top! A shocking discovery.

His smile vanished and hot jealousy surged through him. What man? Was she dreaming of a man from her past? Or someone in her present she kept secret from him?

Clenching his fists, he left the room and closed the door. From his side of the door, he knocked hard several times.

"Sarah, get up. It's time for breakfast. I'm going down."

Chapter Six

"What are your plans for tomorrow and Sunday?" Sarah asked on Friday night.

They had made it through the first week. But many months were ahead of them before Brent received his inheritance and the title to the house. Too early to let down their guard and claim victory. She worried about Mr. Stone. The dinner had gone much too smoothly. Lawyers were a suspicious lot, weren't they? Still it would be nice to relax for a few days.

"Hmmm. Haven't given it a thought." Brent turned to the sports page, relaxed and content. This was the pattern of their nights together. He was pleased that Sarah shared his taste in music and books. Often the TV wasn't turned on. There were spells of companionable silence with no need to fill it with words or noise.

"Why don't you play golf or go to your exercise club or whatever men do to get away from their wives."

"I don't play golf, nor do I belong to a health club. Since I've never been married, I have no idea what

78

husbands do to get away from their wives." Sarah scowled at his impish grin. "Maybe I don't want to get away from my wife."

His teasing caused her cheeks to turn a delightful pink. "Stop that. Get serious. What did you do before you married me?"

Brent stretched his long legs and lounged back in his chair, studying Sarah from under half-closed lids. "On Saturday I try to sleep late, have brunch and spend the afternoon in the pool. How does that sound to you?"

"We'll follow your routine. I'll join you in the pool. Since there was no one here during the week, I couldn't take a swim."

Brent's pulse quickened at the thought of Sarah in a swimming suit. To see her bare shoulders and long, beautiful legs as she dove into the water and swam across the pool. Would she ask him to put sunblock on her back?

"What else do you do?"

"Huh? Oh, dinner, dancing, going to a party. On Sunday I often go to garage sales, flea markets or antique shows."

"Garage sales! You? Why?"

"You never know what treasures you'll find. It's fun and a challenge."

"Oh sure," Sarah scoffed, "and what treasures have you found so far?" Her treasures at garage sales had been used clothing for a fraction of the new price. Well, no, she still had the crystal perfume bottle from a bygone age.

He walked to a side table and picked up an old autograph book covered with red velvet and trimmed in gold. "Here's one, and those porcelain figurines of a shepherd and his flock are another. Want to come with me?"

"I'd love to." To be with Brent she'd even go to a boring lecture!

He said, "Tomorrow I'll knock on your door to let you know I'm awake."

The next morning Brent awakened at his usual time. He puttered around his room. He knocked on the connecting door. "Sarah, I'm starving. Are you ready to go down?"

"Just a minute." When Sarah opened the door, Brent gave a low whistle. A long, pale pink satin negligee enhanced her soft curves. A delicate lace nightgown peeked from the neckline. She tried to stifle a yawn.

He ran his fingers through his hair and looked frantically away from her. Over her shoulder, he saw her bed was already made.

The reminder made him walk to his bed and punch the other pillow before making a jumbled mess of the bed clothes.

"Come into my parlor, said the spider to the fly," he said, making a low bow and putting his hand over his heart.

Sarah's hand fluttered to her throat. "W-what do we do now?" Uncertainty shown in her eyes.

"Why, darling," he said softly, "Don't you want to toss a nightgown on the floor?"

"Of course not!"

He walked toward her and she took a step back. He put a finger under her chin, raising her face so he could look into her beautiful brown eyes.

"Don't worry, I'm not going to kiss you," his finger caressing the line of her chin before he dropped it.

Why was he flirting with her? Sarah was only his contract wife. After she left, he had other plans for his life. Yet, it was so easy to forget.

Brent lounged beside the pool, a book opened to a random page, not seeing a word. Behind his dark glasses he watched the woman who was making a shambles of his orderly life. She wore the bathing suit they purchased in Arlingford. He secretly imagined her in a red bikini. However, she chose a black one-piece, not cut too low in front or too high in the back. And she looked fabulous in it.

He flung his glasses on the table and dove into the pool, coming up beside her.

"Bet you can't beat me to the end—"

She had already taken off, swimming strongly, her laugh floating back to him.

"You don't play fair, Sarah Victoria Chambers!"

He admitted defeat. They clung to the edge of the pool.

"So, what's my prize?"

He planted a quick wet kiss upon her smiling up-turned lips and ducked her head under the water.

Sarah surfaced, sputtered and coughed. "Brent! Is drowning me my prize?" She wouldn't think about the kiss right now.

"What? You don't like your prize? Next time, play fair."

While they lay in the sun, they talked about many subjects, from politics to the chances the United States had in the coming world swimming competition. On some, they agreed; on others, their disagreement was hot and decisive, with no chance for compromise.

Sarah enjoyed the afternoon. Being married to Brent

was nice. But this wasn't a normal marriage and she had to stop thinking it was. She rose to her feet and pulled on her robe.

Brent turned over on his back and looked up at her in surprise. "What's the matter? You're not leaving so soon?"

"The sun's getting to me."

"I'm sorry. I should have watched out for you. Are you going to be all right?"

Sarah felt like a worm. Here she was, lying again, and so easily. She longed to confess her falsehood, but didn't.

Brent walked her back to the house. "Take an aspirin and have a nap. We'll take a drive into the country and have dinner out. Okay?"

Sarah nodded and escaped. Brent didn't want her for his real wife. The prenuptial contract said so. Sure, they were getting acquainted and talked to each other in an agreeable fashion. But she had to fight the growing attraction which drew her to him like a magnet. She thought of the year ahead. Though Brent was willing to overlook her background, she doubted others would be so tolerant. It was easy to imagine Ashley looking down her patrician nose at her!

After Sarah retreated, Brent dressed and went into his study. He looked at the contracts he needed to prepare for the meeting on Monday. For the first time, work didn't interest him. Sarah's enchanting and winsome face kept coming between him and the sheet of numbers. When his uncle was alive, they spent many hours, day and night, going over financial and corporate reports. Only after he became engaged to Ashley did he make time for a social life. Not enough, apparently. It would be different with Sarah at his side.

The weekends would be devoted to social activities and getting closer to each other. He longed to be with her every minute he was home. His lonely study no longer drew him inside.

Sarah. His contract wife. His wife. No, go back to the previous clause. His contract wife, in-name-only.

He carried on a silent argument with himself. Getting emotionally involved with a woman who would leave him at the end of a year was foolhardy. And wasn't *he* the fool who had made that timetable?

Besides, she wasn't suitable.

Of course, she was. She was intelligent, capable and utterly adorable.

But they had so little in common.

Rubbish. Look at how well they were able to talk to each other on every subject every day. And she made him feel happy to look forward to each day.

Unfortunately, she was determined to be a business partner only, and not a wife.

As soon as Sarah came down the stairs, Brent was ready to go out for the evening. The afternoon had been endless for him.

"We'll drive along the Sunberry Trail. There's a rustic inn which serves delicious steak sandwiches. It's been run by the same family for over one hundred years. You'll love it."

"Sounds like it's a favorite of yours." It pleased Sarah that Brent wanted to share it with her.

Later, after they finished their sandwiches and a thick slab of homemade apple pie, Brent fed quarters into the juke box. When the strains of a slow, country western song filled the room, he held out his arms.

Sarah went into them gladly and wound her arms around his neck. She tucked her head under his chin and listened to the hammering beat of his heart. It felt so good to be held once more by warm arms . . . his arms. She knew it was foolish to want his arms around her forever. Forever? A year was all she had.

All too soon they drove back.

"Thank you for a lovely evening, Brent."

"We'll do it again," he promised.

Sarah slowly walked up the stairs in a bemused state. Why did he have to be so nice? Why did she allow his charm to overcome her common sense? They were only business partners and nothing more. Was the prenuptial contract really embedded in concrete? Surely something in the coming year would shatter it to pieces and let love—no. Such wishful thinking would only make it harder for her to walk away at the end of the year.

Rain lashed against the windows the next morning and continued to fall all day. The wind moaned around the corners of the house and rattled the shutters.

Sarah had been looking forward to going treasure hunting with Brent, but there would be no garage sales today. Another hard gust buffeted the house. Sarah was thankful this was an ordinary rain. Thundershowers, with their crashing thunder and lightning flashes, frightened her. This childish fear made her ashamed and she tried hard not to let anyone know of her fright.

The atmosphere in the house became oppressive. Sarah shivered and left her post at the hall window. She took her book into the living room and curled on the couch.

Earlier, Brent had gone into his study. He didn't stay long. He prowled around the living room. His answers to Sarah's attempts at conversation were barely polite.

Well, well, thought Sarah. *What have we here? A spoiled little boy angry because his plans had been foiled?* She'd better get him out of the house.

"Brent."

"What?"

"*Casablanca* is playing at the little theatre on Fifth and Elmwood. I'd like to see it again."

With his attention, she went on, "We can have a spaghetti supper at a darling family restaurant that's nearby. I can vouch for it because Johnny—because I've been there many times."

"Johnny?"

"That was years ago."

Sarah silently cursed herself for that slip of her tongue. She didn't want to explain about Johnny tonight. To top it off, she had aroused Brent's curiosity—or was it jealousy?

"What do you say? It's a miserable day and a movie is ideal for this kind of weather."

"May as well." Brent wisely didn't pursue the subject of Johnny, but it wasn't forgotten.

Running from the car and across the restaurant parking lot, Sarah tilted the umbrella handle. The rain dripped down the collar of Brent's jacket.

"Hey! Watch it!"

"I couldn't help it. The devil made me do it!"

Brent laughed. "Just as I thought."

"Sarah!" Mr. Lorenzo cried happily. "We haven't seen you for a long time. Come, come, sit down and I'll serve you our special dinner."

"This is my husband, Brent Chambers. I've been telling him about your fabulous pasta."

"I'm so happy to meet you." He looked fiercely at Brent. "You take care of our Sarah. She's special and deserves to be happy once more."

"Don't worry. I know how special she is and I'll make her happy."

If only he could make his promise come true. Later, she realized her memories of being here with her first husband hadn't spoiled this evening with Brent. Her life was going forward, and she knew Johnny would approve.

Laughing and holding hands, they dodged the raindrops again on their way to the movie.

During the movie, Sarah shared her popcorn with him. Brent's fingers touched hers when she reached into the large container at the same time. It seemed an intimate encounter in the dark theater which made her catch her breath.

"Mmm. This is good, isn't it?" Sarah asked, hiding her reaction to his casual touch.

"Ambrosia from the gods," he agreed, a touch of irony in his tone. And feeling angry at these gods for throwing him a curve: he wasn't supposed to develop tender feelings for his contract wife.

As she would do to her brother, she punched his shoulder, "Oh, you!" When his arm encircled her shoulders, she moved closer to him. It was natural to progress to putting her head on his shoulder for the rest of the movie. This much touching was allowed, wasn't it?

When the final scene came, Sarah gave a sniff.

"Crying?"

"It's so sad. The ending always makes me cry."

He raised her face and wiped her tears away. His "silly goose" had no sting in it.

* * *

On Monday morning Henry Stone called Sarah.

It was the call she had been expecting and dreading. She hadn't been as confident as Brent that they had nothing to fear. Henry knew Brent's history, but not hers. If only she had told Brent about Johnny. With such a large fortune at stake, a lawyer would be suspicious of a little nobody and investigate her past— and wonder why the first marriage had to be kept secret.

"Yes, I'll be in your office at ten o'clock."

Sarah debated calling Brent but decided against it. Why have him worry when she, hopefully, could handle the matter herself.

Henry didn't keep her in the dark for long.

"Why didn't you include in your employment record that you had been married before?"

The cross-examination had been nerve racking. He finally accepted her explantion. She was still mourning the sudden death of her husband at the time she applied for the position; to have people question her was more than she could endure at the time. To leave it out of her record didn't affect her ability to do her job. Since then, it wasn't important to tell personnel about it.

Henry asked, his shrewd nose ferreting out something amiss, "Does Brent know these facts?"

Sarah stammered, "No—no, he doesn't."

"Why not?"

"It never came up and I didn't want to make him unhappy at the time. We were in love and nothing else was important." Sarah stared defiantly into the cold eyes of the lawyer. She reiterated, "My past will in no way affect my present marriage to the man I love."

"You do intend to tell him, however?"

"Now that you have brought it up, I see that it is important and I will tell him." To herself she amended the statement: *When the time is right.*

When Brent came home, Sarah told him she had been to see Henry because he wanted to know more about her past.

"Was he satisfied?"

"Oh, yes. We got along just fine. Nothing for you to worry about." She was trusting Henry not to talk to Brent.

Her interview with Henry and going to Lorenzo's opened her Pandora's box. Since Sunday, unwanted memories assailed Sarah. Her unhappy past rose to haunt her. It drove her to return to her old apartment after lunch on Thursday. Brent didn't know she continued to pay the rent on it. The list of things he didn't know was quickly growing!

Their marriage had a whole year to go. What if something happened to end it before next May? At least she'd have a place of refuge.

Entering the apartment, she sat on the narrow window seat and drew her knees up to her chin. Wrapping her arms around them, she laid her head down and let her thoughts drift . . .

Brent.

He wasn't at all like Johnny, in looks or temperament. It had been love at first sight with Johnny, who was always laughing and so loving. When he suddenly died, she wanted to die, too.

He was in Memorial Hospital for routine testing—not for a life-threatening condition. The autopsy showed a heart weakened by childhood rheumatic fever and complications from diabetes.

Even today, her eyes filled with tears and her throat ached at the memory of that terrible morning telephone call. They had only six deliriously happy months together. Though poor as the proverbial church mice on their combined part-time salaries, they both attended college. Their poverty didn't matter—they were together in this, their love-nest.

She still wanted to keep this part of her life safe from questions. She didn't know Brent well enough to feel secure about his reaction. Had she deliberately neglected to tell him in his office because she didn't want him to use this knowledge to reject her as a candidate?

Sarah held her head in her hands. She was so mixed up. She no longer knew what was really going on in her head and her heart. And until she did, she wasn't going to tell Brent and take the chance of upsetting their fragile relationship.

Before she locked the door, she gave the place one last look. It was just a lonely, empty apartment—no longer her home. This surprised her. She was glad she had come back to see it and put her memories to rest. Her place was with Brent. In the coming year she was going to guard her heart. Having lost her beloved husband without warning, she feared falling in love again, and certainly not with a man who had no love for her. A sometimes arrogant, domineering man—who was going to be home before long and expect his loving wife to be waiting for him!

"Taxi!"

* * *

Brent looked forward to coming home now at the close of a stressful day. No longer did he enter an empty house; Sarah waited for him.

Her presence pervaded the house. The servants were cheerful. Furniture was moved, ugly bric-a-brac disappeared and vases of flowers were everywhere. Their marriage of convenience was going well . . . so far.

Brent's euphoria was pricked on Thursday. He called the house to ask Sarah if she wanted to see the old production of *Pride and Prejudice*. He knew she was an old movie buff and admired Laurence Olivier and Greer Garson.

His housekeeper said, "Mrs. Sarah called a taxi after lunch and left the house. She's not back yet."

Brent swiveled his chair to look out the plate glass window of his office.

Sarah.

She was never far from his thoughts.

A taxi. Why hadn't she called Symes? Without warning, ugly questions bombarded him. *To keep her destination a secret? To go to Johnny? Had it been his pajamas she wore to bed? Who was he, anyway?* She had said "That was years ago," but he had seen the pain in her eyes before she shut it out. He must have been important to her once—was he still?

He broke out in a sweat at the thought of Sarah in the arms of another man.

No, Sarah had gone shopping. She'd probably come home with an armful of packages. He smiled, remembering her last shopping trip. Sure, that's all it was. Foolish of him to doubt her.

Sarah waited for him as usual, with a hug that was tighter than usual and lips that lingered on his cheek. He said, "It's wonderful to have you here every night."

A warm glow flooded Sarah. Even though her mind told her this was all an act, her heart continued to rejoice in every show of affection.

Later, when Sarah said nothing about her activities, Brent asked, "Did you have a busy day?"

"Not too busy. I did try to visit a friend but no one was home."

There, thought Sarah. She hadn't lied. Johnny never would be home. Sarah turned away from Brent's speculative gaze. She blinked quickly to prevent the birth of tears. She rubbed her forehead. "I've got a headache. If you don't mind, I'm going to take an aspirin and go to bed."

"Good idea. Hope it will be gone by morning."

"Thank you. At least it's not a migraine this time."

After Sarah left, Brent's thoughts troubled him. Was she avoiding questions about her visit and the name of her absent friend? Or was he making a big deal out of a friendly visit? Sarah was free to see old friends. Their contract didn't require her to report her every action to him.

But . . . he wished she'd confide in him. After all, she was his wife. Why was he feeling so depressed tonight? She could never be more to him than what they had agreed on in the contract. They were together for mutual benefit and nothing more. Yet thoughts of Sarah's absent friend bothered him for the rest of the evening.

Brent remembered Sarah's words on their honeymoon. He snapped open the black velvet box. The beautiful solitaire diamond ring sparkled in the light. He muttered, "Another stage prop as Sarah suggested!" But, deep inside, he wanted it to be more than a prop.

Putting the box in his pocket, he went down to breakfast. He pondered the right time to give the ring to Sarah.

A romantic candle-lit dinner?

Much as the idea appealed to him, he rejected it. Nothing romantic about their involvement. Recalling his proposal ("Look over this contract") he winced. Sarah even had to tell him to buy this ring. His hard-earned business acumen had failed to foresee the innumerable pitfalls and obstacles in a marriage of convenience.

He could hand the ring to her at the breakfast table and say, "As per your suggestion, here it is." Would his feisty wife freeze him with a disdainful look?

His final decision was, "Tonight, after dinner."

Sarah stood by the window, watching the twilight deepen into a soft darkness. A new moon, a sliver of silver in the deep blue sky, hung near the horizon. A night bird sang his final song. Lost in the beauty of the scene, she jumped when Brent spoke to her.

"We're going to walk down to the gazebo, Sarah—now." He grasped her arm firmly and urged her toward the door.

His imperious manner annoyed Sarah. She wanted to dig in her heels and refuse his order. A better way came to her.

"Yes, my lord and master," she replied, her eyes cast down as she made a curtsey. Though Brent gave a snort of annoyance, he kept propelling her along the garden walkway.

In the gazebo he paced back and forth. Sarah sat

quietly and waited. At last, he sat beside her and pulled the box from his pocket.

"I should have bought this earlier. Sorry to be so late." He snapped open the box. Even in the dim light of the gazebo, the hidden fires trapped in the many facets of the diamond solitaire flashed.

"Oh, it's beautiful!"

He reached for her left hand and slipped on the ring. His lips brushed a kiss on her hand before he slowly dropped it.

Sarah's heart raced with the magic his romantic gesture ignited. Her lips parted and she swayed toward him. He bent down to touch his mouth to hers. It was gentle, warm and undemanding.

The sudden warmth generated by it made her heart trip over itself. Waves of happiness surged through her. When Brent kept her wrapped in his strong arms, her pleasure intensified.

A warning intruded into her euphoria. Brent hadn't given the ring to her from any romantic desire. He had remembered her taunt about buying her a diamond ring. She abruptly broke away from him.

Brent drew in a ragged breath. The warm rush of feeling generated by the kiss still coursed through him. Her sudden withdrawal bewildered and hurt him. He listened to Sarah's cool compliment.

"The ring is gorgeous. I'll be happy to wear it this year."

Brent hid his disappointment. The kiss, which had wreaked such havoc to his world, had meant nothing to Sarah. His answer to her statement strummed with cold resentment.

"The ring is yours—not just for a year. Do you understand?"

"Of course. Shall we go back to the house?"

Brent followed Sarah, feeling depressed and unsure of himself. He shouldn't care that his kiss hadn't stirred her as deeply as it had him. Though his male ego had been pricked, there was a deeper reason for his disappointment. It was better Sarah had the sense to keep their relationship on an even keel.

Still . . . it had been an earth-stopping kiss . . . so different from the obligatory kisses for the benefit of the servants. It promised what could be . . . he would like to repeat it very much.

Chapter Seven

When Sarah came up to her bedroom after breakfast, her first installment check lay on her dresser. She picked it up and looked at it for a long time. She had wondered how she was going to be paid—for she was working, wasn't she? Instead of her cramped computer cubicle, she was in a mansion, surrounded by every luxury and four servants. It was only a matter of degree. If it wasn't for the marriage license, she could easily be Brent's mistress, being paid for services rendered.

They were married, and for a whole month. How quickly time passed. The days had been mostly heaven, but with enough trouble to keep her on her toes.

It was mostly of her own making. She couldn't control her feelings and emotions. No matter how hard she struggled, she was drawn to Brent. His smile made her nerve endings quiver and his good nature made it easy to live with him. He wasn't the cold, aloof man she had observed in the office. Oh, no, it would be easier if he was! Sometimes she thought he, too, was having trouble keeping their relationship impersonal.

She had a checking and savings account in the name of Sarah Gordan-Chambers. When the year was over, it would be easy to drop the name of Chambers. But how could she drop her feelings for Brent out of her life? A divorce, a slip of paper, could never wipe out her memories of this man who was coming to mean so much to her.

She also wasn't going to berate herself about being paid this money. Without her help, Brent would have gone bankrupt and many people would be unemployed. The money paid to her, this month and for the next eleven months, made her wealthy beyond her dreams. She could do all kinds of things for her family, as well as have her college education financed. She'd start going full-time, starting in September. By next May, she'd have her degree in Business Management and many more business opportunities would open to her.

She'd grovel at Brent's feet if necessary (well, when he wasn't looking!). In the meantime, she'd smile and kiss and hug him whenever it was necessary to prove theirs was a loving marriage. And she'd keep a tight rein on her feelings.

This first month hadn't been so hard. She'd just have to arrange the rest of the year to fall in line as easily.

On Saturday, a week later, the scene at the breakfast table was relaxed and peaceful. Sarah enjoyed her third cup of coffee while trying to decide if she wanted to go shopping for school clothes so early in the season.

A pleasant routine had been established and now flowed effortlessly. They went out to dinner, to the movies or browsed in flea markets and antique shows. When they attended the required fund-raisers and social functions, Sarah learned to ignore the speculative glances of his acquaintances. Being dressed in the latest fashion and Marcus' hairstyle gave her self-confidence to stare down the critics. Brent was unfailingly attentive and did his best to protect her feelings. She appreciated his efforts. It did, however, make it more difficult to remember his attentions weren't grounded in real affection. To get his inheritance and his house, he had to play his part successfully.

"Darnit!" Brent exploded. Sarah's gaze went to the letter in his hand. He had captured her rambling thoughts.

"Bad news?"

"It's Aunt Hattie. She's coming for a visit." Consternation and dismay furrowed his brow.

"Oh, Brent," Sarah laughed with relief, "It can't be the end of the world, a visit from your aunt. Why are you so upset?"

"Though she means well and has always had my best interest at heart, she is a domineering, pig-headed, opinionated, stubborn woman. She'll meddle into every part of our lives and make trouble for us. And she prides herself in being outspoken."

"You're exaggerating. She can't be that bad."

Brent gave a scornful snort. "To make it worse, she looks like an angel. She's petite, has white hair and an innocent, sweet expression. But I warn you in advance, this is a diabolical cover-up."

Sarah burst out laughing. Brent glared at her and tossed the letter across the table to her. "Here, read it

yourself and see what she says about you. You won't
laugh then."

My dear Nephew,
   *I am disappointed in you. To think I had to
learn of your marriage from Henry Stone. When
were you going to tell me?*

Sarah exclaimed, "You didn't tell your aunt you got
married? I don't blame her for being upset. How could
you?"

Brent had the grace to look ashamed. "I meant to
but I forgot. I was hoping we would have more time
to perfect our act."

Sarah shook her head at him and turned back to the
letter.

*What happened between you and Ashley? We all
expected this perfect marriage. Why a hasty marriage to one of the hired help? I can only assume
she tricked you into it. It won't take me long to
get to the bottom of this.*
   *At any rate, please pick me up at the airport
on Tuesday afternoon at four. I fly on United.*
                              Your loving Aunt,
                              Hattie Rutherford

A flush stole over Sarah's face as she read. However, when she lifted her gaze from the letter, amusement glowed in them. A delightful laugh bubbled out.

"You're right, she's a character. She'll make life a
merry circus."

"I'm glad you can see humor in this visit. I'm
dreading it."

"Come on, she does have some reason to be suspicious, Brent. How long do you think she'll stay?"

"Depends. My uncle and she fought constantly. When she realized she couldn't get her way, she'd leave in a huff, and we wouldn't see her for ages."

"We can't have her doing that. Are she and Henry Stone good friends?"

Brent gave a groan. "I'd forgotten they went to school together. He's probably planted Aunt Hattie here to spy on us."

"He'd never be so underhanded—to have you lose your inheritance. Your aunt is curious, that's all, and wants to protect you. She'll look me over with a magnifying glass."

Brent's gaze ran over her like a caress. "You have nothing to be worried about. You'll pass her inspection."

"Her visit will be a real test for us. There's nothing we can do until she gets here."

When Hattie Rutherford walked briskly through Gate 12, Brent watched her mincing walk. She wore a long, double-strand of jet black glass beads. He'd forgotten she always wore them. On previous visits, he'd been glad to hear their warning click. It gave him time to scurry out of her sight.

On the way Brent tried to keep his aunt talking about what she had been doing since she last visited. She, however, was too shrewd.

"So, young man, you got married without me. What was the big hurry?"

"I fell in love and couldn't wait a moment longer."

Hattie gave him a scornful look. "Do you take me for a fool?"

"Of course not, but that's the way it happened." Brent looked into his aunt's eyes boldly.

Hattie smiled at him. "I shall see."

When Brent hoped the inquisition was over, she murmured, as though talking to herself, "Your wedding was May tenth. And you came into your inheritance on the fifteenth."

Brent didn't answer her and sighed with relief when they arrived at the house.

When Brent drove up to the door, Sarah flung it open. Before his aunt could speak, she said, "Welcome to our home. Brent is so pleased you came for a visit. I'm Sarah."

Hattie's gaze took in the dark green dress with its demure white collar and nodded her head. "At last we meet. I'm glad to be here."

Sarah endured Hattie's sharp perusal. Then she smiled and picked up a small overnight case.

"I'll go with you to your room. Brent, bring up the rest of the luggage, please." She said to Hattie, "You've come at a good time. The gardens are at their best."

At dinner Brent told his aunt the news about her old friends. Sarah answered the questions about her family and volunteered her plans for going to college and getting her degree.

"I don't understand. I hope you aren't going to be one of those career women who feel they must work. You're married now and should devote your time to Brent and having a family."

"Oh, no, I won't go to work. But I believe in finishing what I start and I want to have the joy of completing my education. Brent, the darling, wants me to do what makes me happy. We'll still have time to start a family after I graduate."

Aunt Hattie filled her plate. "Sadie is still a good cook. This meal is delicious." She gave Sarah a deceptively sweet glance. "What changes have you made in the staff?"

"None. They have always satisfied Brent. Since I haven't any experience in running a large household, I depend on them to do it."

"Good. You have common sense, young lady."

Aunt Hattie ate some more. The food could have been sawdust for all Sarah tasted. She looked at Brent. He wasn't helping to make conversation or steer his aunt away from her questions. After all, they were in this together.

Hattie turned her attention to Brent. "What happened with Ashley?"

"We had personal differences we couldn't resolve. She didn't want to live in Brighton and I wouldn't move."

"Wasn't your wedding to Sarah a bit sudden?"

Brent reached over to grasp Sarah's hand.

"We had a whirlwind affair and wanted to be married right away. It's been lonely without Uncle Matthew, and Sarah's family lives miles from here. There was no reason to wait."

Apparently satisfied, at least for the moment, Hattie questioned Brent about his business until dinner was over. Brent suggested they take a walk through the beautiful gardens.

It was a short one for Hattie. "This has been a long day for me. I'm going to bed, but you lovebirds may continue your walk without me."

Sarah wasn't sure if her "lovebirds" was sarcastically said or not.

Sarah waited until she could no longer hear the click of the beads before she gave a big sigh of relief. "I thought we'd never be alone."

Brent put his arm around her shoulders and gave them a squeeze. "You've been wonderful. How do you think it's going? I know she's suspicious."

"We'll have to be very careful."

They completed their stroll to the edge of the river in silence. "I could learn to like your aunt. She's shrewd and intelligent. I'm sorry we have to be dishonest with her and Henry Stone. They're honorable people of the old school."

Brent nodded. "I've always tried to be honest and sincere. And now I've dragged you into this. If you want to stop—"

"Don't be silly. We have to continue. We're in too deep to back out."

Brent found he had been holding his breath, afraid Sarah might take him up on his offer. And then realized his fear wasn't for the inheritance or the house— he didn't want to lose Sarah. Not being able to see her the first thing in the morning and the last thing at night was unthinkable.

He might as well admit to himself he had fallen in love with his partner in a game of pretend! He recalled the exact moment he acknowledged to himself that he loved her. Sarah had entered the living room with a bowl of flowers to put on the mantel for Aunt Hattie's benefit. She had smiled sweetly at him, and he knew he was head over heels in love.

A heartfelt groan escaped him.

"Don't worry," his business associate said, misinterpreting his distress, "We'll be able to act our parts so well Aunt Hattie will never suspect." She gave his arm a lingering pat. "Trust me."

Later, Sarah wasn't so sure. It was feeling less and less like a pretend scenario. Too often, her heart reached out to Brent. She wanted more than a casual brushing of lips or a little hug. That was what Brent expected from her and nothing more.

She gave a moan which strangely sounded like the one Brent had given. Tomorrow was going to be very tricky. How to explain to sharp, discerning and perceptive Aunt Hattie why the newlyweds had separate bedrooms? If they were in England, there would be no question, but they were in America.

Tomorrow she'd think of something.

The next morning Brent turned from his open bedroom door and met his aunt coming down the hall.

He exchanged greetings, hoping she had slept well.

"Where's Sarah? Doesn't she get up and eat breakfast with you?"

"She's downstairs already. She generally talks to Mrs. Ames about the menu."

"She should ask me about my nutritional needs," Hattie complained. "There are a number of things I can't eat anymore."

"By all means, let Sarah know. She wants you to enjoy your stay."

After breakfast, Sarah walked Brent to the door. Kissing him on the cheek, she whispered, "Did you remember to open the door between our rooms?"

"Yes," he said. "I even remembered to take the black nightgown from your room and throw it to the foot of my bed."

Sarah grinned. "You're learning fast."

He laughed and let her go.

With reluctance, she returned to the breakfast room.

"I pride myself on being outspoken," began Hattie.

Sarah's heart almost stopped beating.

"Why do you and Brent have separate bedrooms?"

"We don't," Sarah answered. "Occasionally, I get a beastly migraine headache unexpectedly in the middle of the night. We discussed it and Brent thought the solution would be for me to sleep in another bed. This way I wouldn't have to worry about distrubing his rest. He's so considerate."

Though Sarah thought Hattie wasn't compleltly satisfied with her explanation, she didn't expand on the subject. Besides, Hattie must realize separate bedrooms in large homes were acceptable in many marriages today.

"Let's talk to Mrs. Ames and Sadie on menus. I can learn so much from you." She gave Hattie her most appealing look. "Please, you know there's so much for me to learn and Brent can't help me with household matters. I need to learn from a woman of your experience."

Hattie's response flooded her with relief.

"Come along, Sarah. This will be your first lesson on how to run a household of this size."

Getting ready for work the next morning, Brent heard a timid knock. The connecting door opened behind him. His tie in his hand, he turned in surprise.

"Brent—"

Sarah leaned against the doorway for support. She wore a wispy pale pink chiffon nightgown which clung to her. Her golden-brown hair was an untidy cloud about her white and drawn face.

Brent sprang to her and with gentle hands urged her to lie down on his bed.

"What's the matter?"

"It's a migraine headache. If I was a superstitious person, I'd say I brought it on myself because of the story I told your aunt yesterday."

"Don't be silly, Sarah. No one knows why a migraine comes on. When did it start?"

"After I went to bed."

"You've been up all night?"

She nodded. "I took the four pills I had left of my prescription. It didn't help. I need to have my prescription refilled." Sarah held out the empty bottle.

"As soon as possible." He pulled the covers up to her chin. "Rest in my bed for now." Brent appreciated the irony of having her in his bed for the first time—without him!

Sarah sighed and closed her eyes. She heard his steps fade away. She snuggled down. Of course her lie to his aunt hadn't brought on the headache. The need to make-up stories was getting harder and harder. How much easier it would be to just fall in love. As she drifted off into a light sleep, her last thought was this would be the only time she would be in Brent's bed.

Later, the clicking of Hattie's beads announced her presence by the bed.

"My dear, I brought your pills." Hattie gave her the medication and held the glass of water to wash them down. "You rest and I'll take care of everything. I've had migraines and rest is the only cure."

* * *

The migraine was gone by morning and life became normal again. If one could call it normal with Aunt Hattie, it seemed, everywhere at all times of the day. The click of her beads heralded her approach, and warned Sarah and Brent to hold hands or plant a kiss on the cheek.

In the weeks following Hattie's arrival, Henry Stone became a frequent visitor and dinner guest. The two of them seemed to be in a conspiracy to harass the "lovebirds" with innuendo, sly looks and nudges.

"We'll go now and leave these two alone . . ."

"We're sure you want to go to bed early to-night . . ."

The Fourth of July picnic brought this comment to really torment Sarah: "It will be so nice to have the patter of little feet around this old house . . . We may celebrate more than our nation's birthday next year."

A baby, she thought, *a darling, kissable baby with Brent's jet hair and blue eyes . . .*

Being expected to gaze adoringly at Sarah tested Brent's control. Pretend. Only to her—to him it was real. If he or Sarah managed to find separate activities, Aunt Hattie was there to pull them together. Respite was too short. The bedroom doors were kept locked so Aunt Hattie couldn't burst in with an "emergency" in the middle of the night and find them in separate beds.

Brent didn't know how long he could take this. He tried working later at the office, but found he was only punishing himself. He missed being with Sarah.

He wanted a real marriage. All the reasons why he shouldn't love her were unimportant now. What a joy it would be to have her love him back, to openly flaunt their love before the eyes of Aunt Hattie and Henry.

* * *

Sarah was also frustrated. She had looked at Brent at breakfast on Sunday morning and her cup dropped onto the saucer. She loved this man! Her pretend husband had vanished and she wanted the real thing. Gone forever was her vow never to fall in love again. Love had intruded as suddenly as it had with Johnny. And, if she were honest, she had fallen in love with her boss at first sight when she had gazed into his blue eyes from across the room many months ago.

He had stood by his office door, wearing a dark gray suit with an air of authority that made him seem bigger than life—very much a man a woman could depend on. He had looked up from the papers in his hand. His gaze scanned the busy office until it met with hers. Everything melted away. She felt as though she were floating, with the earth no longer under her feet. She thought "I've fallen in love." He had gone back into his office, leaving her bemused and bewildered at this turn of events.

And in the next breath she denied it. And she came to believe her denial for the ensuing months.

But because of Aunt Hattie's interference, her love had broken out-of-bounds. Her problem was now increased a million times. How was she going to keep pretending? An impossible situation—impossible!

It was no wonder she was in a black mood. Listening to Hattie's chatter didn't help to dispel it. If only the woman would take off those everlasting, irritating beads with their click, click, click!

She had to get away. She called a cab.

"Aunt Hattie, I'm going to visit a friend today."

"Who is this friend? Is it a man or a woman?"

Sarah was shocked and irritated. "I don't think that question deserves an answer. There's my taxi!"

Sarah marched out of the room, feeling enormous satisfaction at seeing the open-mouthed Aunt Hattie being denied the chance to have the last word. Hattie's chest heaved in agitation and the beads swung wildly from side to side.

Sarah went to her secret refuge, her old apartment. It welcomed her with open arms. She made herself a strong cup of tea.

For the first hour she enjoyed the freedom from Hattie's scrutiny. Then the apartment started to haunt her.

She picked up a picture of her first husband taken at the beach. She had always adored Johnny's smile and the love that showed so clearly in his eyes.

Did she sometimes see it briefly in Brent's eyes? The kisses, the warm looks . . . was it all pretense? How she wanted him to love her as much as she loved him.

She remembered something her grandmother always used to say, "It's easier to get into something than to get out of it." She should have listened to her. What a mess she'd gotten herself into—and for a whole year. She'd made her bed and now she'd have to sleep in it.

At two o'clock Brent called and asked for Sarah.

"She's not here," his aunt answered. "She went to see a friend. She wouldn't tell me if it was a woman or a man."

"Aunt Hattie, my wife doesn't have to answer to you. When she comes back, would you tell her I called? Nothing important."

Brent resisted the urge to slam down the phone. Annoyance at his aunt's words was partly responsible; the other was the sharp suspicion and jealousy that raced through him.

Sarah gone—for the second time. What if she were with another man? Johnny? He clenched his hands. The thought of her being with someone else tore him apart. He knew so little about Sarah's past. Why hadn't he asked important questions at the time he made his business offer to her? Like a fool, he had been too focused on getting married to any woman who would have him under the circumstances.

Brent paced the floor of his office. At this late date, did he have a right to know the details of her life? Ordinarily, a husband could ask questions, but their situation wasn't normal. And he didn't want to hear the wrong answers if he questioned Sarah. He'd wait for her to tell him herself.

Why had he thought a marriage of convenience would be a simple and uncomplicated answer to his money problems? He tried not to listen to the little voice in his head that reminded him he wouldn't have Sarah otherwise. It had never really been strictly business . . . as he well knew.

On top of everything, he had to face nosy Aunt Hattie. How to persuade her to cut short her visit? Not an easy task since she had entrenched herself in their home, endlessly watching them. With those infernal clicking beads.

When Sarah met him in the hall on his return from the office, Brent said, "I called and Hattie said you had gone to see a friend. Did you enjoy your visit?"

Sarah brushed his cheek with a kiss. "It's always good to see an old friend. No one you know."

She wanted to tell him the visit was to her old apartment, but Aunt Hattie was there. She didn't want to explain in front of her and face her inquisition and advice.

They weren't alone the rest of the evening. The next morning, it was the same story. The look of speculation in Brent's eyes wasn't lost on Sarah, or Hattie. Sarah had the uneasy feeling Brent had been seething with questions inside, but he didn't ask them. Could he be jealous?

Aunt Hattie continued her visit and made no mention of a possible departure. She seemed to be enjoying herself. She renewed old friendships during the day, but she was home every night to keep them company.

While Hattie was with her bridge group on Wednesday, Sarah made her plans. She called Brent.

"I need a Hattie-break. There's a Shakespeare revival at the Idlewood Playhouse in Mayberry. It's only a four-hour drive from Brighton. Friday is the last performance of *Othello. The Tempest* starts on Saturday. Want to go?"

"Are you kidding me?"

"I've already made the reservations. Please be home at noon on Friday."

"I jump to carry out your every command," he teased and hung up.

Brent waited in vain for his aunt to question him about their weekend getaway. He raised his eyebrow at Sarah. She didn't look at him. Ah, he surmised, she hasn't told the woman.

This time, Hattie was out-maneuvered by Sarah. At eleven o'clock on Friday morning, Sarah informed

Hattie that Henry had been invited to dinner that evening.

"How nice. I enjoy Henry very much."

As soon as Sarah heard Brent arrive, she said to Hattie, "Brent has been working too hard. We have a wonderful opportunity to get away for the weekend to see a Shakespeare revival in Mayberry. Here's the address of where we will be staying if you need to get in touch with us."

Hattie's mouth opened wide to make a protest. Sarah raced on. "We're leaving immediately. Henry will be here for dinner, so you'll have company. Such good friends can find something to do while we're away."

Brent appeared in the doorway.

"I've just told your aunt about our good fortune."

From the pursed lips and the frown on his aunt's face Brent saw her displeasure. He carried on, "We are still newlyweds, you know. Anyway, I wouldn't be suprised if Henry is glad to have you to himself." This last was an unxpected hit. A blush began to dye Hattie's cheeks.

Brent smiled at her. "You look beautiful when you blush, Aunt Hattie. I'll bet Henry thinks so, too."

In confusion, Hattie twisted her beads into a knot. "Don't you think you two had better hurry along?"

"Yes, ma'am. I'll run up and get our bags."

Chapter Eight

The drive on Skyline Parkway to Mayberry was restful. The absence of tractor trailers was a welcome relief. The low mountains, green with pine trees and stark cliffs of rugged stone, painted a pleasing picture.

"Turn here." Sarah looked up from the map in her hand.

"Twilight Motel" was on the sign. Brent's eyebrows shot up and a low chuckle rumbled out of him. It would be a new experience for him to stay in a place with a name that conjured up all kinds of ideas.

Sarah looked straight ahead.

"Ah, yes, Mr. and Mrs. Chambers. We're so happy to have you with us. Bellboy, please take their bags to cottage ten. You'll have complete privacy."

Sarah knew Brent's eyebrows rose again on hearing the word "cottage." She squared her shoulders and headed down the path. When Brent whistled softly the almost forgotten tune of "Just a love nest, cozy and warm," Sarah's cheeks burned. She admitted the name did evoke such a picture.

Brent kept on whistling until the door closed behind

them. He carried the bags into the bedroom of the cottage. He gave a loud chuckle and said, "History repeats itself, eh, my dear? I'm experienced at sleeping on a couch."

"This—this was all I could get at such short notice," Sarah stammered. "We can try to find something else tomorrow."

"What, and leave this beautiful cottage and our privacy? I don't think so," he teased.

He reached out and gently stroked her cheek. "You got us away from Aunt Hattie and for that you deserve a gold medal."

An understanding was reached.

"No talking about the past or the future. We're going to have fun this weekend. Okay?" Sarah asked.

"Fine with me. Let's go shopping. When we drove in, I noticed some interesting little shops." Brent had become quite fond of shopping.

He bought Sarah a handcrafted silver bracelet and she fastened a thin turquoise necklace around his neck.

"No man wears a necklace," he protested.

"See, it says right here, it's guaranteed to bring you good luck." She looked slyly up at him and a small smile curved her soft lips. He couldn't refuse anything Sarah asked on this lovely evening.

Their enjoyment of the performance of *Othello* far exceeded their expectations.

On entering their cottage for the night, Brent ordered with a smile, "It's late. Off to bed with you." He suggested, "Tomorrow we'll go to the museum and take a ride into the mountains before we see *The Tempest*."

"Good night, Brent. Thank you for a fabulous day."

Brent watched her enter the bedroom and close the door. Regret and disappointment flooded him. This time away from Aunt Hattie should have been filled with days of delight and nights of fun.

Making his bed on the couch, he cursed his stupidity for negotiating a marriage of convenience with a little clerk who'd always caught his eye. It galled him to admit the emphasis on his money problems had been a smoke screen for the real reason. Now he didn't know how to blow it away.

The next day, whenever Sarah laughed or teased him, he felt rewarded for his efforts to make her happy. At the evening performance of *The Tempest*, she sighed with happiness and laid her head on his shoulder. His hand engulfed hers and held it tenderly.

Early Sunday morning they left Mayberry with regret. They dallied on the way back, stopping in small villages to look into the shops to admire and buy the local craft items.

"I don't know where you're going to put all this stuff," Brent remarked.

"In our big house? Don't be silly."

Brent's heart gave a flip of joy. Sarah had said "*Our* house." With this small word of encouragement, she'd made his day.

Aunt Hattie greeted them with a big smile. "I'm so glad you're back. I hope you had a good time."

Sarah hugged her and kissed her cheek, and knew she had come to love this woman. She had helped her to feel confident about managing a staff and the affairs of the household. When all was said and done, their performance for Hattie's benefit made her admit that she, Sarah Victoria, had fallen in love with her pretend husband. As long as Hattie was in the house, she would be able to enjoy Brent's touches and kisses.

When Brent first asked her to *pretend* to love him for a year, she had wondered if such a thing was possible. Now she knew how impossible it was. She was faced with a new, bigger lie: to hide her real love.

One week later, Hattie left to attend a wedding, thus finally bringing her visit to a close.

"Do come back soon," Sarah begged, in all truth. "You've been such a help to me and I'll look forward to your next visit. We love you."

The house was strangely quiet. Sarah missed listening for the warning click of Hattie's jet beads and the stimulation of keeping one step ahead of her. Brent's attentions had dwindled to a brief hug and a peck on-the-cheek ritual. How wrong she had been to think it was more than an act for Hattie's sake.

The building of Brent's mega-store in the Brighton Shopping Mall was finished. He worked many long hours to stock it and to prepare for the grand opening. He was never home and she missed being with him. There were no more intimate evenings spent together.

Seeing the deep, tired lines on his face and the slump of his shoulders, one evening she suggested, "Let me help. I can stock shelves. Art supplies aren't heavy." She laughed. "I'm really good at lettering signs, too. I minored in Art and loved it."

Brent had looked at her as if she had sprouted two heads. "No wife of mine is going to stock shelves! I have ample employees for that type of work."

She felt left out of his life with each passing day. Brent made no attempt to suggest anything she could do to help him or involve her in his business. Involve her? He didn't even talk about what was going on like he had before, or mention if he had any problems. In fact, he seemed to have forgotten she had ever worked for him at one time. She wanted a place in his life. She wanted to become indispensable to him, and *not* because it would advance her career.

At heart, she wasn't a career-driven woman. To marry and have a family was her desire. When Johnny died, her dream of a family life had died with him. After the tragedy, she knew she would have to support herself and had thrown all her efforts into taking college courses at night. A degree would give her a chance to make a better salary and forge a place in the business world. Studying filled her empty hours.

After college, she and Johnny had planned to work side-by-side in his computer company until they started their family. Even then, she would have a part in his business.

She wanted this with Brent—to have him ask for her input and depend on her support.

The next evening Sarah tried again.

"If you don't want me to work in the store, can't I come back to the office? There must be so much more work because of your expansion. I could at least do my old job."

"No!" roared Brent in outrage. "Are you out of your mind? How do you think it would look if my wife—*my* wife—went back to her old job? If you insist on working, I'll find something for you to do with me—" Brent stopped, appalled at what he had just said.

Sarah in his office, in the same room, with him? For of course he couldn't let her work in the outer office, or even outside his door.

Work with him, side by side? He wanted this nightmare picture to disappear. He had enough trouble seeing her every evening, when he ached to take her in his arms and kiss her. But be with her all day *and* during the evening? Only a glutton for punishment would do this.

For a ghastly moment Brent had a vision of Sarah sitting behind his desk while he took orders from her. He suspected she was competent enough to do just that! He was already going to be devastated when she left his house at the end of the year. Now she would always haunt his work space as well.

Sarah threw her arms around his neck and hugged him. "That'll be wonderful. With my computer skills and the courses I've taken so far, I know I can do anything you need done. You'll see, I'll be your right hand."

Brent's brows came together in a frown. The die had been cast and he was in for it. He said, "It'll take a day to get a desk moved in and a computer and phone set up."

"I understand. I'll be ready to go with you the day after tomorrow."

Her delight was so great, Sarah wanted to dance out of the room and up the stairs. She was going to be with him day and night. No longer would she be useless and lonely. However, one look at the storm clouds hovering over Brent made her contain her excitement. He was sorry he had made the rash proposal. She didn't care. Her heart's desire was being fulfilled. She wasn't going to let him off the hook. When he no longer wanted her in a few weeks, he'd admit she had been a great help to him in his hour of need. And that he'd ask her again if an emergency ever arose before next May.

Next May.

All joy left her. She kept forgetting she was in his life for a limited time. Oh, if she could only become so important to him, in his company and in his heart, that he'd never want her to leave him.

At the breakfast table two days later, Sarah looked covertly over the rim of her coffee cup at Brent. He appeared to have had a bad night. He swallowed his tomato juice in one big gulp and scowled into his coffee cup. Indications he didn't want her to go with him today were in every line of his body.

Too bad. This was for his own good, and he'd acknowledge it in due time. Seeing her in the red suit he disliked deepened his scowl. The suit was her armor. She had to be chic and sophisticated, in command of herself before her former co-workers. For a moment, she trembled and her self-confidence took a nose dive. How were they going to react? What stories had been passed around when the news of her marriage to the boss had become known? It didn't matter what they thought. She was thankful Brent had let it be known she was coming into the office today.

She was even more grateful to have his arm around her waist when they exited the elevator. Every eye turned to them.

Sarah smiled up at Brent and then waved to the group in general. Brent did the same. Sarah took a deep breath and threw back her shoulders.

To Sarah's relief, spontaneous applause erupted. Obviously, collective opinion was in favor of her "promotion."

"I'll join you in a few minutes," she said. "I want to talk to some of my friends."

As Brent entered his office, he heard her laughter and realized she hadn't laughed a great deal in his house. He vowed to think of ways to make her so happy she wouldn't want to ever leave him. His life would be dark without her and he couldn't bear thinking about it. Restless, he stared out the window.

The door opened and Sarah came in, her flowery fragrance drifting to him, tantalizing him.

"That wasn't so bad after all," Sarah said. "It was clever of you to tell them yesterday."

Brent shrugged his shoulders. He didn't feel clever—nervous was more like it. How was he going to keep his mind on business with Sarah working at the desk next to his? He pointed to the desk.

"Hope you'll be comfortable and able to work here."

"This is perfect." Sarah sank into the high-backed leather chair at her desk. She gave a gleeful laugh and spun around. At Brent's astonishment, she apologized, "I always wanted to do that. My old computer chair had a defect and wouldn't let me spin around."

Suddenly, Brent felt happy. He was going to savor having Sarah and her sunshine with him for whatever time they had. He smiled at her and she smiled back. He yearned to take her in his arms and kiss her. To assure her he wanted her to be with him.

"What did you want me to do today?" Sarah asked, taking a deep breath. She was happy to see his smile. She wanted to believe he was glad to have her here with him.

"See if you can contact the Environmental Protection Agency," he said and placed a folder in front of her. He explained, "I decided several weeks ago to stop buying lead-based paint. Although I know it's dangerous only if used on dinnerware, I don't want to stock it in any paint used for arts and crafts. No use in taking a chance someone will be poisoned."

"What's the problem?"

"The paint is in my warehouse. I've tried to get the Environmental Protection Agency to give me a date when I can take it to them and have them dispose of it. Try calling them again. I need the space for the new paint I've ordered.

"I'll do my best." Sarah opened the file and familiarized herself with its contents. She saw the notations of attempted calls. They were hard to pin down. Sarah reached for the phone.

Brent motioned to her that he had to leave and left a note on her desk with a phone number. Sarah waved to him and blew him a kiss.

Brent's eyes widened in surprise and he didn't know how to react to such a simple gesture. Didn't he know he was to catch it and send it back to her? Apparently this was the first time anyone had blown him a kiss. She accepted his crooked smile into her heart. Poor Brent. She would have to remember his background. All her life, it was so natural for her family members to hug and kiss and give pats of encouragement. She recalled she had been the one to initiate most of the casual physical signs of their love in front of his aunt—except for the kissing. That he did very well on his own. A warm glow suffused her from head to toe. Her only complaint about his kisses were their infrequency!

Sarah called person after person at the Environmental Agency. She doggedly refused to let up. This was the only job Brent gave her to do and she was going to succeed.

Before noon, Brent returned. Sarah was hanging up. She gave him a big smile and thumbs up sign.

"I did it! I finally did it!"

"Tell me. I need some good news."

"The Agency will take your paint if you can deliver it to them on Wednesday morning."

"You got them to do it?" Brent found it hard to believe. "What did you do, cast a magic spell? I haven't been able to get the time of day out of them."

Sarah confessed, "I listened to Mrs. Arnold's family problems first before I make my request."

"That's wonderful. You deserve a good lunch. Let's go."

After lunch, Sarah asked with a teasing smile, "Okay, boss, what impossible job do you have for me to do next?"

"Okay, Wonder Woman, get a list of all the companies who manufacture lead-free paint for crafts. I did order some from a company in Dallas but I need more suppliers."

Sarah looked closely at the sly smile on Brent's lips. Was he just giving her busy work or was this important to him? She'd soon find out. She wanted to help him so much, to become an integral part of his life, both in this office and in his heart. If only she could do it in the next few weeks.

By four o'clock, Sarah had a list of fifteen suppliers. She swung away from her computer to talk to Brent and found his gaze on her. Her breath caught in her throat at the longing mirrored in his eyes. In a moment, he looked away and she wondered if she had been mistaken. Longing? Why had she interpreted his gaze with that adjective? Since Aunt Hattie left, an awkwardness had come between them. Brent's kisses had been mere pecks on the cheek or forehead and his arm around her was stiff as a board. He acted as though he didn't want to touch her.

Today had been no different. Though they were working side by side, Sarah felt the gulf between them. Oh, he put on a show for the office when they walked through to go to the elevator—his arm around her waist, tucking her closer to him. But back in the office, he immersed himself in his work and didn't speak except to tell her where he was going and how long he would be away from his desk. And he was out of the office more than he was in it.

Sarah hid her disappointment and hurt behind a smile. Brent hadn't wanted her to come and work with him. She should have listened to him. But she had accomplished something he hadn't been able to do with the Environmental Protection Agency. And she had gathered an impressive list of suppliers. These results he couldn't fault.

Sarah handed Brent her list. "What next?"

"Good work, Sarah. Dictate letters to each company asking for their spec sheets and price lists. Also their delivery schedules. If the grand opening of my store draws in as many customers as I hope, I'm going to have to order soon."

After she returned to her seat, Sarah asked, "Brent, explain. If business has been so bad, why didn't you sell the lead paint to someone? I assume you're losing money having it disposed by the Agency."

Brent looked uncomfortable. "I considered that option but dropped it. If I didn't want to endanger my customers, why should I let someone else do it? I'd rather take the loss and be able to sleep easy."

A surge of pride swept through her. So, money really wasn't everything after all. Brent was an honorable businessman in an age when this was very rare. She wanted to praise him but his look stopped her. She nodded her head.

"I'll get busy right away. Will we be working late? If so, I better call Mrs. Ames."

"Until the usual time. I don't want you to get tired on your first day."

"Tired? Me tired?" Sarah protested. "Let's keep—"

"No." Brent couldn't sound more imperious.

A quick rush of resentment flooded Sarah. Just when she began to think he was so wonderful, Brent had to throw his weight around. Sarah opened her mouth—then closed it. Why make an issue of a minor matter? Actually, she was ready to go home.

"Yes, sir," she said, bowing her head. She peeked up at him through her lashes and held back a laugh at the sight of the indignation causing him to frown. She quickly began to type and ended the tension between them.

Two weeks later Brent's office was back to one desk. He turned his back to the emptiness, and looked moodily out the window. Sarah's tenure had been bittersweet.

He couldn't fault her ability and her work. She had overcome all obstacles to every problem he gave her. She even revamped the medical benefits for his employees. She also convinced him it would actually be cost-effective to put in a child daycare center. On her last day, the women had a luncheon to express their appreciation for her efforts on their behalf.

His work load was back down to normal, and the store had opened to great fanfare. Business was brisk.

This was the sweet side of the ledger.

On the bitter side was the transformation of his wife into a cold, efficient, dynamic businesswoman the instant she stepped through the door of his office. She tossed cool, little smiles his way from time to time, but no physical contact. None whatsoever.

In every way she reaffirmed she was only his business associate. All the warmth of their forced intimacy under the eagle eye of Aunt Hattie was gone. He had been a fool to think Sarah was beginning to care for him.

Worrying about how Sarah would greet him that night bothered him all day. For two weeks they arrived home together with no reason to impress the servants. While he had fallen in love with his wife in-name-only, his dearly beloved was determined to abide by the letter of their agreement. Everyday she made this clear to him.

When he entered the entrance hall, no Sarah was there to greet him. Nor was she in the living room curled up with a book. Brent's disappointment was greater than he cared to admit.

The garden door flew open and Sarah ran down the hall to him. Her hair was windblown and her cheeks red with exertion. Her breath came in gasps and perspiration ran down her face and soaked her green jogging suit.

She threw herself at him and apologized in gasps, "I'm sorry Brent—my watch stopped—I so wanted to be here as usual when you came home."

He pulled her to him and kissed her. Two weeks of frustration melted away. How could such a sweaty creature smell so fragrant, how could salty lips taste so sweet, how . . . he gave up wondering and just enjoyed.

She drew away, gasping and smiling.

"Please have Mrs. Ames hold up dinner for twenty minutes. I have to shower and change."

She ran up the stairs.

Brent felt weak with relief. He felt like jumping in the air and clicking his heels together. His Sarah, his mercurial, unpredictable, elusive Sarah was back. The gods were indeed smiling down on him today.

Chapter Nine

The next morning, Brent's good-bye kiss was warm on Sarah's lips and hope raced through her. Her imagination created an idyllic scene of Brent carrying her up the stairs, his lips never leaving hers until she gasped for breath. He said, "My dearest darling, I love you, I love you, I love only you. I can't live without you . . ."

Her head full of fantasy, it took her a moment to focus on the installment check lying on her dresser.

Of course, today was August fifteenth. Brent never forgot. In July, Aunt Hattie had been visiting. With weightier matters on her mind, she had quickly deposited it, not giving it a second thought.

It was different this morning. Since her stint in Brent's office, they had fallen back into a warm and relaxed relationship. They talked easily about this and that and found much common ground. It felt as though they had always lived together. To get her heart racing, Brent had only to breathe! How she loved him. If only some magic would make their contract disappear and she would be free to tell him she loved him.

The check was a sledge hammer designed to shatter her foolish dreams.

Fool, fool, fool! Will I never learn? Why do I keep forgetting I've practically sold myself to Brent? I'm his employee, not his wife!

She threw herself face down on the bed, arms covering her head. Tears trickled slowly down her cheeks. A little over eight months until the end of the assignment. The check reminded her she had entered willingly into this marriage—for money. Her heart was ready to admit the *real* reason she had married Brent: she had fallen in love with him and dreamed he would fall in love with her during this trial year.

The check poured icewater on her hopes. A cold reminder of their business deal.

Sarah dried her tears and dragged herself to her desk. Her mail needed to be sorted. She eagerly snatched the fall/winter catalog from Brighton University and carried it to her small balcony.

As she sank into the white wicker chair drawn up to the round glass-topped table, she sniffed the crisp air. Fall would soon be here in all its spectacular glory. She loved fall even though it signalled the coming of winter. But then, she mused, she liked that season, too.

Thankfully, Brent paid for the business courses she wanted to take. Her gaze skimmed the pages. Excitement strummed through her. By taking extra classes she would be able to graduate at the end of the coming May. A full year before she could have done it if she was still taking classes only at night. What a heady thought! Her goal of being economically secure was within her reach.

She should be singing with joy, but her elation fell

flat. A career in business no longer held charm for her. She wanted to be a full-time wife and mother.

Sarah planned her schedule. Advanced Accounting. If she took it, she wouldn't be home at dinnertime, two nights a week. Not good, but it wasn't offered at any other time this semester. She wouldn't be home to greet Brent with her wifely hug and kiss. Would he miss her? Perhaps that would be a good thing.

She had time to register today.

Several hours later, a full schedule faced her. Although she remembered Brent had said he would buy her a car, she leased a compact car with her credit card and drove it home. It felt good to be independent. Her checking account showed a healthy balance. She had never been so rich in all her life.

Brent sensed a difference in Sarah. Her welcoming kiss barely brushed his cheek. She didn't look into his eyes in the usual mischievous way. Neither was she her chatty self during dinner.

"What's wrong, Sarah?"

"Let's take a walk and I'll tell you."

After she seated herself in the gazebo, Sarah didn't act in a great hurry to talk. She looked at the velvet-green sweep of the lawns to the rose gardens. A wispy mist rose from the river and dusk was deepening. The crescent moon sat low on the horizon.

Brent waited for her to speak.

"I registered for my fall courses today."

"Good. You've been at loose ends since you helped me in the office. You'll need a car."

"I've already leased a car."

"Why did you do that? You know I planned on buying you a new car, a safe car, not one that's been driven who knows how many miles, and may be in dubious condition."

Sarah tossed her head and her eyes darkened with resentment. Was Brent belittling her ability to take care of herself? His attitude disappointed her.

"I have the money you've paid me. I'll pay my own way and make my own decisions. I've abided by the terms of our employment contract!"

Sarah's choice of words took Brent by surprise, an unpleasant one. "I had no idea you felt this way. Please be assured I won't hinder your plans," he said, his voice cold and his lips pursed to a thin line. "I appreciate all you have done to fulfill our agreement." He stood up. "We should walk back to the house. You're trembling with chill."

He took off his coat and draped it around her shoulders. Sarah wanted the earth to open up and swallow her. Her choice of words had hurt him and she wished she could recall them. She pulled the jacket more closely about her. It was still warm from his body. If only his arms were enfolding her.

"Thank you." Without saying more, she started walking, blinking back the tears.

Brent followed silently.

In the hall, she slipped out of the jacket and murmured a low "Good night." Brent nodded and went into the dining room.

Going to the side board, he poured himself a brandy. Sarah's words "employment contract" shocked and hurt him. Had she considered him only as her employer all this time? Never as a husband? Never with affection? Hadn't they been getting closer and reaching out to each other? How could he have been so mistaken?

In his bedroom, he stopped before his dresser. He glanced idly at the schedule of classes Sarah had left for him. She was taking a full program. His gaze fell on Advanced Accounting, six to nine o'clock every Monday and Wednesday night. It meant she would be walking across the campus in the dark to the parking lot and driving home at night. By herself.

Brent paced the floor. Didn't Sarah know how dangerous the campus was for a lone female? It was impossible for the campus police to be everywhere at the same time. He wouldn't allow it!

He banged on the connecting door.

"Sarah, open up! I want to talk to you."

He waited impatiently, his exasperation rising with every bang.

"Sarah, open up!"

Brent's loud commands pulled Sarah out of the shower. Dread filled her. Something terrible had happened. She grabbed a blue satin robe and slipped it on without stopping to dry herself. She threw open the door.

"What's wrong? Did Mrs. Ames have an accident?"

"I've been looking at your schedule and . . ." Brent stopped talking.

He wanted to pull her into his arms, to kiss her until she filled with rapture.

He stepped back. Just in time he saw the apprehension in Sarah's eyes.

He turned away, stumbling over his feet. "Never mind. I'll talk to you in the morning."

He slammed the door shut and took great gulps of air. Thank goodness he had recovered his senses in time. Tomorrow was plenty of time to discuss the schedule.

As it had been since the beginning, a good night's sleep wasn't there for him.

On the other side of the door, Sarah's knees gave no more support than wet noodles. She sank to the floor, wrapping her arms around her bent knees, and laying her burning face on them. All she could murmur was, "Oh, goodness, oh, gracious."

A shuddering sigh shook her. She had been about to throw herself into Brent's arms. Thank heavens Brent had stormed back out. She dried her hair and got into bed. Try as she could, she couldn't think of an answer to the question, "What had made Brent so angry and upset?"

Brent pleaded an early meeting with a supplier the next morning. "We'll have our discussion tonight."

Sarah wandered to the garage after lunch. She debated going for a drive in her new car. It looked so small and disreputable next to the polished town car. She saw Symes put down the hood of her car.

"What are you doing, Symes?"

He flushed with confusion. "I didn't expect you."

Sarah was intrigued. "Well?"

Symes discomfort increased. "I'm sorry, but Brent didn't want you to know. He asked me to check over your rental to make sure everything's okay."

A warm glow of happiness filled Sarah. Was that what was bothering him? What an absolute darling. When she told him about the lease, she had been so horrid to him. Here he was, looking out for her welfare. If she hadn't surprised Symes, she wouldn't have known.

"What's the verdict?"

Symes wiped the grease from his hands and listed the things he didn't like. He finished by saying, "The rental company did lease you a usable car that meets inspection, but you must remember it's not like a new car or one which had only one owner."

Sarah thought for a moment. "I'll be right back."

On her return from the house she asked Symes, "Will you return this car to the rental company for me? Here are the papers." She added with a smile, "Don't tell Brent. It's our secret."

"Sure thing. But what will I say when he asks me tonight?"

"Tell him you're still checking it over. I'll tell him before we go to sleep."

Symes smiled. He knew about the effectiveness of a wife's pillow talk.

Brent surprised Sarah by taking her to Lu Fong's for dinner. Sarah laughed at her unsuccessful attempts to eat with chop sticks. "Brent, how do you do it?"

"Practice, my dear, practice."

Afterwards, they walked along the wall bordering the Waddy River. Stopping to watch the water flowing noisily over the rocks, they leaned on the stone parapet.

Finally, Sarah asked, "All right, what was bothering you so much last night?"

Brent took a deep breath. "Could you change your schedule and take Advanced Accounting earlier in the day?"

"Why?"

"Look, I don't want to interfere, but it isn't safe for you to be crossing a dark campus at that hour."

Sarah didn't look at Brent. She leaned over to see

the little falls near the parapet. She recalled the many times in the past she had been frightened. She dreaded hurrying across the campus after her night classes. It would be just as dangerous this fall.

She remembered the reason she added the course to her schedule. Upset about the implications of the installment check, she wanted Brent to suffer. Since then, she had put her pettiness behind her. She was going forward with her life, without her foolish dreams of a fairy tale ending to this year.

"Sarah?"

"I can do without the course this semester. I'll drop it."

The big smile which lit up Brent's face was the reward she wanted. He had been afraid for her, and probably dreaded another burst of temper from her.

Easy conversation filled their time together. Later, they walked up the stairs together. At her door, Sarah smiled.

"Good night. I've enjoyed this evening."

She opened the door, started through it, hesitated and then said, over her shoulder, "Since you weren't happy about my leased car, I had Symes return it this afternoon."

The door closed before Brent could say a word.

Brent walked into his room in a daze. Never would he be able to anticipate what Sarah would do next. Wasn't life with her wonderful and amazing! Someday, he vowed, he'd convince Sarah he wanted to be her real husband. To change the "only for one year" to "forever."

At Sidle Motors the next afternoon, Sarah balked. "I don't know anything about new cars. You pick one, Brent."

"No. This is your car. Come on, let's look around."

Sarah's brows wrinkled in a frown. These cars were very expensive. Why hadn't Brent taken her to a compact car salesroom, at least? If she had suggested he get her a used car, she could imagine his reaction! What a wreck of a car she and Johnny had bought and hand-painted black in order to cover the rust spots. But they were so happy with it, laughing every time they got into it. How different her life was today. She was going to have a new car.

Urged by Brent to make a choice, Sarah picked a pretty blue sedan, which turned out to be a Mercedes. She shuddered to think of the cost, but consoled herself by vowing to leave it behind when the year was over. She didn't dare to voice that decision aloud to Brent. He was looking so pleased with himself for buying her the car.

September fifteenth.

Brent laid Sarah's check on his office desk. He didn't know what to do with it, not after her outburst last month. "Our employment contract."

The last thing he wanted was to be Sarah's employer. When she spit out those words at him, it shocked him to the core. A husband didn't employ a wife. And he was her husband. The marriage license said so. The bottom line, also, was that he had fallen in love with his wife. That she hadn't fallen in love with him or considered him her husband didn't alter the situation.

What to do about the check? If only he had arranged for it to be deposited directly into her account . . . but back to his problem. If he didn't give it to her, she might question him. After all, it *was* her money as stipulated in their contract. But what would he say?

"Sarah, you're not employed by me. You're . . ." *What was she? My dear, dear, unobtainable love, my wife.*

"Sarah, here's your check as per our agreement . . ."

"Sarah, I forgot to put this on your dresser . . ."

"Sarah, I hope . . ."

"Sarah . . ."

Darn. He'd give it to her tomorrow. He'd delay disturbing the calm and peace that had been restored. Everything was fine between them.

As Brent got ready for bed that night, he admitted that the peaceful condition of his marriage was only on the surface. He had to fight a constant battle with his desires and his yearnings. So many times he wanted to shake Sarah out of her sweet, adoring wife act, and make her aware of the feelings raging in him.

He wanted to shout, "Look at me, Sarah. I'm a man, not a marriage contract. Want me a little, hold me, love me."

The connecting door separating them became the focus of his frustration and longing. He wanted to get an ax and chop it down. The door drew him like a magnet. It was the first thing his gaze went to when he awoke. It was the last thing he saw at night.

Tonight, his frustration boiled over. He couldn't do anything about the door, but he could make sure he didn't see it mocking him the last thing tonight.

Sarah heard the thuds and thumps coming from Brent's bedroom. An object fell to the floor. The sound of breaking glass made Brent swear in an inventive and colorful fashion.

She wanted desperately to find out what was going on, but Brent's language didn't invite her inquiries. She'd have to stifle her curiosity until morning.

Brent said nothing at breakfast. In fact, he seemed to dare her to question last night's activity in his room. She blandly passed him the toast.

After he left the house, she raced up the stairs and into his room, closing the door behind her.

She burst into hoots of laughter, tears starting to run down her cheeks.

He had changed the furniture. Why was the bed angled away from the wall, placing it almost in the middle of the room? Well, it was now facing the windows.

What would the servants say? Since a man never changed the furniture around, she'd have to take the blame. Should she say they wanted to see the moon rise? Was there a moon last night? Could they even *see* the moon on this side of the house?

The door opened behind her.

"Mrs. Sarah!" Mrs. Ames' voice was almost a shriek. "Whatever happened here? If you wanted the bed moved, you should have told me. And you broke the beautiful lamp Miss Hattie gave to Brent."

Sarah was all apologies. "I'm sorry. I tried to convince Brent not to do this last night, but you know how stubborn men can be."

Mrs. Ames was slightly mollified. She shook her head. "Why is the bed facing that way? The head of the bed should be against the wall, the way it was."

"Brent and I wanted to see the moon."

"What moon?" The housekeeper wasn't finished. "You'll have to explain to Miss Hattie about the lamp. She set great store on it."

"Yes, Mrs. Ames." Sarah fled downstairs.

At dinner Brent looked uncomfortable, but he still didn't speak about last night. He could see Sarah was having the greatest difficulty keeping a straight face and carrying a casual conversation about the weather and world news.

She finally said, "Mrs. Ames wants to know when you will be picking out a new rug for your bedroom. The faded areas in the rug can't be covered with the present furniture arrangement."

Brent could feel the flush spreading from his neck to cover his face. He got up from the table. "Please tell Mrs. Ames I don't want a new rug."

As he strode hurriedly out of the room and toward his study, Sarah softly called after him, "I told Mrs. Ames we wanted to watch the moon rise." And she burst out laughing.

Brent slammed the study door. *Well*, he thought, *that is as good a story as any. Leave it to Sarah to save the day.*

Watch the moon.

His room was on the wrong side of the house! But wouldn't it be wonderful to have a room where the moon could be seen, with Sarah all cuddlesome and warm to watch it with him?

Darn the whole situation. This new arrangement would be as frustrating as looking at the door. More so.

He'd move the bed back.

When Sarah snuggled down to go to sleep, she had a fit of laughter. Then another memory made her situp abruptly. She hadn't been given her installment check. This was the sixteenth. She could understand Brent being remiss, what with all his problems with his furniture. She giggled again. Even so, he was so dependable.

She got out of bed and searched all around the dresser. Had it fallen to the floor or dropped into the top drawer?

She couldn't find it. It would surely be there tomorrow. How she hated being reminded of the kind of marriage she had, especially when she longed for it to be real.

Stop being such a fool, Sarah. Fantasy doesn't create reality.

The next day she avoided her room until after lunch. She put it off as long as possible. Keeping her gaze on the rug, she walked to the dresser.

The hated check was there—but a beautiful red rose lay on top of it.

Sarah danced around the room, holding the rose to her lips and breathing in its fragrance. Wild, happy thoughts tumbled in her head. Had Brent meant this to show that he valued her as a person—even cared for her? A red rose had so many romantic connotations, didn't it? Whatever the reason, the rose took away the sting of the check's meaning.

Chapter Ten

The reports for the third business quarter covered Brent's desk. He still had a pile of work to do. Everyone had left for the day hours ago.

When the phone rang, he yanked it out of its cradle. "Brent Chambers speaking," his voice sharp, unhappy to have his concentration interrupted. He wanted to finish and go home to Sarah.

"Brent, darling, you don't know how good it is to hear your voice again."

It took a moment for him to recognize the caller. "Ashley! When did you get back? I thought you were on an extended honeymoon."

"I'm at the airport. Oh, Brent, I have to see you. I'm so unhappy. When I left you and married Thornton, I made the biggest mistake of my life."

"What? What's going on?"

"I've filed for divorce."

No way was he getting involved in Ashley's marital woes.

"Ash, I'm sorry things haven't worked out for you, but you walked out on me. As far as I'm concerned, you made your choice and you have to work it out."

"Brent, Brent, please don't shut me out," Ashley sobbed. "You're the only one I can turn to. Besides, I've never stopped caring for you. Surely you haven't forgotten how much we've meant to each other all our lives."

"No, Ashley, it's over and I won't stir up dead ashes. Call one of your other friends." Brent's voice was hard. "I have a lot of work to finish before I can go home. I'm going to hang up."

Of all the people to come back into his life, it had to be Ashley. It hadn't taken her long to throw out poor old Thornton.

Now she wanted back into his life, and even expected him to come running after her. At one time, her sobs would have brought him to his knees. Her voice no longer attracted him and whatever feelings he'd felt for her had died. He realized he hadn't given her a second thought since he married Sarah.

His brows knit together. Was her ego so big that she was ignoring the fact he was now a married man? Perhaps, in the happy throes of her brilliant marriage, she hadn't paid much attention to the news of his marriage. But now that she had filed for divorce—could she be thinking that he should join her in a similar action? Did she remember the terms of the will? Would she make trouble? He shuddered at the possibilities. He knew what Ashley was capable of when she wanted something.

But there was nothing he could do about it tonight. No use thinking about it. His reports had to be finished.

At home, Sarah counted the chimes of the mantel clock. Ten o'clock. Brent hadn't worked this late in a very long time. She couldn't sit still. Books and magazines had been leafed through and dropped. They were getting along so well and enjoyed their evenings together; more and more it felt like a real marriage. The house was a mausoleum without Brent. She wished he'd come home.

The raucous buzzing of the doorbell had her running from the living room. Brent must have forgotten his key.

So sure it was Brent, Sarah didn't think to be careful and swung open the door, a smile lighting up her face. "Forgot your—

Her mouth dropped open and her eyes widened in surprise. Why was Ashley Kirkland Bixley visiting at this hour? Or visiting at all!

Ashley looked Sarah up and down, taking in the black leotards and her pink T-shirt. The look of distaste she gave Sarah set her teeth on edge.

"Is this the new maid's uniform? No matter. I'm Ashley Kirkland, a very old friend. I'll just go up to Brent's room." She reached down to pick up an overnight case. "Please don't tell him I'm here. I want to surprise him."

Sarah stepped forward and blocked Ashley's path into the house. "I'm Mrs. Brent Chambers." She drew herself up, regretting she wasn't six feet tall. "And if anyone goes into my husband's room, it will be me!"

"You—you ragamuffin—you can't be Brent's wife! He'd never marry a person like you!"

"He did and I want you out of here."

Sarah glanced out the door and saw the back lights of a taxi disappearing out of the driveway. Darn the woman. She had been so sure she was staying.

Holding her ground, Sarah said in a firm voice, "I'll call you a taxi. I assure you, your wait will be short."

Sarah slammed the door shut in Ashley's astonished face.

Sarah walked to the phone, so furious she could hardly dial. The nerve of the woman!

Ten minutes later, she peeked around the edge of the curtain to see Ashley stomp her way to the taxi and disappear down the drive.

Sarah leaned against the door. Ashley was very beautiful. How was she going to compete with this woman from Brent's past? Why was she here in Brighton? Where was her new husband? She must have known about Brent's own marriage. Yet she had acted so confident of Brent's welcome. Had it been at his invitation? How many times had she come to this house to spend the night? Would Brent remain faithful to their contract marriage? Why should he?

She shivered and rubbed her arms. There were so many things she didn't know about her husband, nor he, about her. How short-sighted the two of them had been when they agreed to marry. To stupidly think it was going to be so easy. The obstacles were increasing almost every day and any hope of a real marriage emerging in the future seemed more impossible than ever.

At 10:30 Brent rubbed his eyes. Too many hours before a computer monitor. The reports were done and the financial growth of his company surpassed his expectations. The infusion of operating money had turned the tide. For that, he had Sarah to thank.

How different she was from his ex-fiancée. He realized he had made a lucky escape. With all its drawbacks, his marriage of convenience was the best thing that had happened to him, and, strangely, felt more "real" than the real engagement with Ashley. Hectic months were before him, judging by the roller coaster ride of the past weeks. Though filled with apprehension and uncertainty, he found himself looking forward to the rest of the year. Brent made a heartfelt prayer that Ashley wouldn't throw a monkey wrench into his life.

When he unlocked the front door, it was eleven o'clock. Seeing the light streaming into the hall, he hurried to the living room. Sarah was curled on the couch.

"Hi, glad you waited up for me." He grinned as she walked toward him. "I like the—umm, outfit."

Sarah flushed with pleasure, his praise wiping away Ashley's hateful remarks. She forced down the lump in her throat and said, "Come into the kitchen. Sadie left a snack."

After eating and taking a refill of hot coffee, he leaned back in the chair. "That hit the spot."

"How's the business done this last quarter?"

Sarah listened with interest as Brent enthused about the increase in sales and the solvency of his company.

"I have you to thank. If you hadn't married me, I would have lost everything."

Happiness flowed over her and she caught her breath at the warmth in his gaze, only to be doused by the memory of Ashley's visit.

"You had a visitor tonight."

"Tonight? Who?"

"Ashley Bixley came to see you."

He sat up straight in genuine surprise. "She did? Here? What did she want?"

"She didn't say. She left immediately." Sarah felt no qualms about leaving out the details. She avoided looking at Brent and turned to put the dishes in the dishwasher.

"Come on, Sarah. What exactly did she say?"

"There's nothing to tell."

Her terse statement convinced Brent he'd hear no more of what had transpired between the two women. That something had, was obvious. And he bet Sarah had been the victor!

Ashley. He should have known better than to hang up on her. She had never given up on anything she wanted in the past. Tonight, she wanted him, wife or no wife in the offing. At this point, he realized he had never known the true Ashley, had never understood what motivated her besides the fun and games of their social circle.

But now he was unavailable. He was a married man and a faithful one, at that. He had a wife who, evidently, knew how to deal with an ex-fiancée.

Brent shook his head. Still, he had a dismal feeling he hadn't seen or heard the last of Ashley. Marriage bonds had never been sacred to her.

Sarah read avidly the items in the newspapers about the activities of Brent's ex-fiancée. Her divorce from Thornton Bixley caused some lurid headlines, but eventually lost news value. Ashley plunged into a whirlwind of fund-raisers and civic affairs.

Some of which Sarah and Brent attended. Ashley always made a point of coming over to Brent, her hand caressing his arm and her body leaning toward him. Sarah she slyly ignored, as though she wasn't at Brent's side. Sarah smiled and never lost her cool. She was cheered by the fact Brent moved away as soon as possible. He placed his arm around her waist and smiled down at her with a loving expression.

Though appreciative of his actions, Sarah worried about Ashley. She was jealous of the woman and distrusted her. She was afraid to question Brent about his feelings for Ashley now that she was back in his social life. What if they were seeing each other in secret? Brent knew he couldn't have an open affair. He had to have a happy marriage for a year, and that meant no hint of a scandal.

Outside of her secret fears and jealousy, Sarah was content with the way their daily activities had fallen comfortably into place. She was busy with her college studies, and Brent's business occupied his days and many nights.

She treasured the evenings he was home. She would curl up on the couch with her assigned reading as Brent pored over a file from the office. By mutual consent they were together as much as possible. The dust, figuratively, settled on her computer desk in her private sitting room.

Often she would look up and find his gaze on her. She'd smile and he'd smile back. Just like an old married couple. They only parted when they went upstairs and slept in separate beds. Sarah hoped Brent regretted the separation as much as she did.

Once alone, however, Sarah fretted about Ashley in the darkness of her room. Oh, she didn't believe Brent would break their contract, but she didn't trust Ashley. She had a sneaky feeling Ashley was biding her time. Sarah guessed Ashley's pride had been hurt badly by Brent's immediate marriage to a clerk from his office. By all reports, happily and lovingly married at that, and only two weeks after she had flown to Paris. That must have rankled her ego, but would it lead to an unquenchable desire for revenge? Sarah felt as though she was waiting for the other shoe to drop with a big thud.

Three weeks after Ashley's unexpected return to Brighton, Brent's call came as Sarah arranged flowers for the house.

"Sorry, but I have to go to Dallas about a paint order. I managed to get booked on the seven-thirty plane tonight. Since I'll be gone for three days, have Mrs. Ames pack my bag. She knows what I'll need. Just a sec . . ."

Sarah heard Brent talking to someone near him. "I'll handle it. Don't worry. There'll be no suspicion . . ."

"Are you still there?"

"Yes, I am."

"I'm going to be held up here until the last minute and won't be able to get home to see you before I go. Have Symes bring my bag to the airport. Sorry, Sarah, I can't talk to you any longer. I hate going away like this. Miss me a little, huh?"

"Of course I'll miss you. Have a good trip."

After hanging up, she felt a wave of abandonment, which was ridiculous. Brent would only be gone three days. It wasn't as though they were lovers who were being separated for the first time in their marriage. Surely this wouldn't be the only business trip he would take. She better get used to the idea, but she didn't have to like it.

She went in search of the housekeeper.

Sarah hadn't heard from Brent for two days. He didn't say he would call, but she was disappointed and hurt that he didn't want to hear her voice or speak to her. Overcoming her pride and reluctance, she decided to call him. She'd ask him when his flight home was scheduled so she could meet his plane.

At eight o'clock the desk at the Hilton Hotel called his room. The phone rang four times before the sultry voice of a woman said, "This is Brent Chambers' room. Do you wish to speak to him?"

Ashley Kirkland!

Sarah hung up the phone very quietly. Ashley in her husband's room?

Sarah laughed bitterly. "Well, well, she got in my husband's bedroom, after all!"

A hard lump formed in her throat and pain burned in her chest. Ashley with her husband, a husband she loved more and more each day. How was she going to stand it?

Memory of Brent's words in the office rushed back to her—"There will be no suspicion . . ."

Clearly, this wasn't purely a business trip. How many more of these trips would Brent take in the coming months? It really wasn't her concern. *He* was the one who wanted the marriage to last a year. But it still hurt! She fought for control. Ashley, a woman she hated! What would she do if he came back from Dallas with Ashley on his arm and ended it all? With business booming and Ashley's own wealth, did he even need his inheritance anymore?

Sarah fought back tears. Though she loved living in this gracious house, with servants and all, the greatest heartache would be leaving the man she loved.

She was thankful Brent would never know she had called. She wouldn't question him about this trip or any other. She would play the part of a contract wife as long or as short a time as he desired. Her resolution didn't stop the tears from running down her cheeks.

While Brent was in Dallas, Sarah slept badly and ate little, causing Mrs. Ames great concern.

Sarah tried to smile brightly. "You know how it is. New brides are very silly creatures, especially when three days seem like an eternity."

In Dallas, it was nine o'clock on the second day away from Brighton. Brent put his pass card into the door slot.

The night was black with storm clouds racing across the sky—a fitting backdrop for his depressing day. He was tired and irritated. It had been frustrating chasing down leads to additional supplies for the lead-free paint his company would be selling from now on.

He wanted to have a shower and hoped sleep would come quickly tonight. He dropped his briefcase on the floor and threw his coat on the living room chair.

He was lonely. He missed Sarah. He was really acting like a new bridegroom who didn't want to be separated from his new wife for one day. He had been captured by those beautiful brown eyes and he loved her radiant smile. He loved everything about her and wanted to be with her right now, instead of miles and miles away, alone in this suite. He gave a deep sigh, taking off his tie. He began unbuttoning his shirt as he opened his bedroom door.

And stopped short.

Ashley lay on the bed. Her honey-blond hair fell in a shimmering wave over her ivory shoulders. She smiled, but the smile froze at the angry tone of Brent's voice.

"What in the world are you doing here, Ashley?"

"I came to be with you as I did last winter. Come and give me a kiss."

Brent made no move toward her. He took a deep breath. "Look, Ash, I don't know how you knew I would be here, but things are different in my life. You broke our engagement to marry another man and I went on with my life. I'm a married man now."

Ashley shrugged her shoulders and held out her arms. "We still can enjoy ourselves, darling. Your little mouse of a wife doesn't need to know," she insisted.

Brent clenched his fists at his side and walked to the door. "Before I say something I'll regret, you better leave. You and I can only be friends—and *only* that. Nothing more, ever. I'll wait in the restaurant until you get out of my suite."

Ashley found her voice. "You—you'll be sorry for this, Brent. *Friends*! You know we're more than that. And you'll always come back to me—"

Brent quietly closed the door. The depth of his revulsion surprised him. To think he'd asked her to marry him. A shudder went through him.

Strange, he hadn't thought of Ashley as a demanding creature before. Only when he compared her to Sarah did this aspect of her character become blatant.

Sarah was so wholesome and good. She stirred him emotionally, but in a different way than he had ever felt. He wanted to put her happiness and her pleasure before his. He longed to hold her and protect her.

He wanted—he wanted what wasn't his.

Well, he'd be home soon. He could at least look, even though he couldn't touch. Kissing her was all he thought about lately. If only things were different.

An hour later, he sprawled out on the couch. He gave a chuckle. He seemed destined to sleep on too-short couches! This time he didn't want to sleep in the bed after Ashley's little stunt. It was so typically Ashley. There was a time he had loved what she did. Now, Sarah occupied his thoughts and his heart.

Brent groaned. He had to stop torturing himself this way.

The three longest days of his life ended and Brent walked quickly into the house. Sarah ran out of the living room, her arms reaching for him, "Darling, you're home!" She didn't look to see if any of the staff was in the hall.

Brent's briefcase landed on the floor with a thud. Delighted with Sarah's enthusiastic welcome, he pulled her close to him. He laughed at her breathlessness and noted how perfectly she fit against him.

Mrs. Ames interrupted them. Brent experienced a letdown. Sarah's joy was for an audience. "So you're back, Brent. We've missed you, especially Mrs. Sarah. She hasn't eaten enough to keep a bird alive."

His feelings picking up, Brent smiled down at Sarah. She was so beautiful, her cheeks flushed crimson and her thick lashes fanning the satin skin.

Mrs. Ames continued, "Brent, you should take her with you next time. You're newlyweds, after all."

"That's a great idea." His answer sent funny little quivers to Sarah's stomach. She'd go anywhere, anytime with him. Being separated was agony. It proved how much she needed to be near him, to know, if he was with her, he wouldn't be with Ashley!

Sarah encouraged Brent to talk about all the aspects of his trip. But not once did the name of Ashley Kirkland enter the conversation. He was keeping their clandestine interlude a secret. Sarah's dreams were haunted by her.

It had become a silent ritual for Brent to leave a flower on top of her monthly installment check. Sarah started a book of pressed flowers: August, a red rose (*did he love her?*); September, a darling little blue forget-me-not (*as though she ever could!*); October, a white, spicy gardenia (*it made her think of moonlight and romance*).

This month, it had been a pink carnation. Its clovelike scent was a perfect lead-in to the Thanksgiving season with her memories of the spicy pumpkin pies her grandmother used to bake. And the comment in the book after she pressed the flower would be: Thanks for this year with Brent.

"Brent, what do you do for Thanksgiving?"

"Uncle Matthew and I usually went to the country club. That way the staff could have dinner with their families."

Sarah was silent and thoughtful. "I think we should invite Aunt Hattie for the weekend. Henry Stone, too."

"You want us to have a traditional Thanksgiving here?"

"Yes. We can still give the staff the day off because I can do the cooking. Aunt Hattie, I bet, would give a hand with the baking. Wouldn't that be wonderful?"

Brent smiled to see Sarah's radiant face. "So now you add cooking to your impressive list of accomplishments?" he teased. "Do I have to worry?"

Sarah gave his shoulder a playful punch. "No, you don't. I love to cook and bake. I was taught by my grandmother and mother. I've missed doing it here."

"You should have said something. I'm sure Sadie—"

"No. We agreed to let the domestic arrangements stand as they were for this year."

In a split second, Sarah had reminded Brent of the true nature of their relationship. He felt the thrust to his heart and his hopes. He pursed his lips.

"Do whatever you want about Thanksgiving," he said. "I have work to do." He walked to his study and closed the door.

Sarah looked thoughtfully at the door. Could it be Brent didn't want to be reminded of their business contract? Was he finding it as hard as she to remember they acted out a charade every day of their lives? But what about Ashley? What was she doing for Thanksgiving? She didn't care. Brent was going to be here with her. It would be good to have a family dinner.

Aunt Hattie was delighted to come. She and Sarah had a wonderful time in the kitchen, working side-by-side. Sarah found she loved her more and more. Henry was his gallant self, paying all the compliments one could desire.

Brent put aside his unhappy thoughts. He even carved the turkey using the chart Sarah obtained from the butcher. And he was determined that there would be another memorable Thanksgiving dinner next year with Sarah at his side as his beloved wife.

Chapter Eleven

And so, November came and went, leaving them with many warm thoughts and memories.

Now December was upon them. Sarah didn't want to acknowledge that six months had also come and gone. She and Brent had moved toward each other such a small distance; at this rate, they would need ten years to become a real married couple. She had no clue how to speed the progress. When she became a little bolder, Brent drew away. If his eyes filled with love, she was the one who fled. It was hopeless.

She knelt at the window seat and watched the falling snow transform the garden into a fairyland of delight.

Christmas was three weeks away. She had already shopped for her family and their packages were shipped yesterday. Arnie and his family were spending the holiday with her parents enjoying the Florida sunshine. Sarah put aside her feeling of longing and homesickness. In the spring she'd invite her family to visit and worry later about what they would think when she and Brent divorced in May.

It had been such a joy to buy big, expensive gifts for them, without looking at the price tag. It was like giving herself a gift.

Thoughts of gifts made her think of her checkbook. It was hard for her to believe the balance. She was so rich. She tried to concentrate on Brent's thoughtfulness in giving her flowers and not just the money. Though she tried not to think about it, and repressed it strenuously, the fact remained. She was in this house and in his life because she was being paid to be here. No matter how beautiful, how intriguing the flower gift-wrapping—it didn't change what was in the package. Wife for hire!

But she wasn't going to dwell on such depressing thoughts. The house had to be decorated for Christmas.

When Mrs. Ames revealed that there were no decorations of any kind in the storeroom or attics, Sarah was upset. She'd get some right away. She got her coat. "Mrs. Ames, I'm going shopping."

"Mrs. Sarah! You're not driving in this weather?"

"Of course. I'm not afraid of a little snow."

"No, no. If he were here, Brent wouldn't let you. It's too dangerous."

Sarah thought a moment. "I'll have Symes drive me. Will that be okay?"

"Much better."

Brent was late getting home. Besides the usual rush hour traffic, the heavy snow earlier in the day had turned to treacherous ice.

He hoped Sarah hadn't taken the car out today. He frowned. He never felt free to come right out and say what he thought or express his concern for her safety.

She valued her independence and ability to take care of herself. Come to think of it, she had never asked for his help since they married. His wife was a very remarkable woman. He was proud of her, but he did wish she would lean on him sometimes.

The car slid sideways. He corrected the skid and concentrated on his driving.

Two beautiful wreaths adorned the double doors. A big ball of evergreens, studded with small white Christmas lights and fluttering red ribbons, hung from the ceiling of the portico.

A broad smile curved his lips and a burst of joy blossomed in his heart. This was Sarah's work, dear darling Sarah who could warm his heart faster than anyone.

Packages and boxes filled the hall, with only a passageway clear to the stairs and the dining room. Sarah had been shopping, no doubt about it.

"Darling, I'm so glad you're home safe." Sarah was radiant, her eyes dancing. "Can you guess what I bought today?"

"I know what's outside. The house looks festive already so why all this?"

She linked her arm with his and drew him into the dining room. "Come on, let's hurry and eat so we can start getting organized for tomorrow. We have the whole weekend to decorate this house from top to bottom."

"Decorate. We have the wreaths on the door. Isn't that enough? That's all Uncle Matthew and I had."

Laughing, she promised delightedly, "When we get through, you won't recognize your own house."

The next morning, the work of transformation began.

Evergreen garlands, with Christmas lights twinkling in them, entwined the banisters and draped the doors and mantel. Mistletoe hung in every doorway. To her delight, Brent maneuvered her under one and claimed his reward. She laughed and went on to place many figurines of Santa Claus on the window sills and in the corners.

The next day Sarah dragged Brent from one Christmas tree to another until she was satisfied with the perfect one.

The tree stood to the right of the fireplace. After a battle with the many feet of lights, everyone helped to decorate it. Every branch and twig had an ornament hanging from it.

"Really, did you leave any ornaments in the stores for other customers?" Brent teased.

"I left a few. Here, this is the last one. You have the honor of hanging it."

"I don't believe it." He took the little red sled and hung it on the tree. It reminded him of the time he found an old sled in one of the sheds. It had been his dad's. A lump formed in Brent's throat. He'd never had the joy of doing any sledding with his dad. If he ever had a son, he'd make sure they did things together.

Sarah took Brent's hand and gave it a squeeze. The finished product was admired by all.

"Just beautiful, Mrs. Sarah."

"I've never seen such a perfect tree."

"I guess I better take the ladder to the garage," Symes said in a matter-of-fact manner.

"Come on, ladies," Mrs. Ames said, "We'll put these boxes away."

Sarah and Brent thanked them. "We couldn't have done it without you."

Brent motioned for Sarah to sit beside him on the couch. The fire crackled and sent showers of sparks up the chimney. "Am I glad it's finished, and," he admitted, "it does look nice."

"Nice? It's fabulous, it's wonderful, it's just what I've always wanted." When she saw the teasing gaze, she blushed, looking like an exquisite rose.

"But we're not finished," she said with a smile.

"What do you mean? I'm exhausted."

"We still have to do our Christmas shopping for the staff's gifts." Sarah's eyes danced with mischief. "You have to come with me. It'll only take a few hours."

"A few hours? It took us over five hours to pick one tree. You go by yourself. Take Symes with you."

"Poor Symes. Aren't you ashamed to put it all on him?"

"No, I'm not."

Sarah sank back and put her head on his shoulder. A perfect way to end the evening, to watch the burning logs sending out firecracker bursts of sparks up the chimney and to dream of a merry holiday.

After dinner on Monday, Sarah quietly took the newspaper out of Brent's hands. "I want you to help me plan your company Christmas party."

"I don't believe in company parties. You worked for me last year, remember?"

Sarah made a face at him. "Yes, I was there. It was the most dismal office in the building. We all thought you were the worst Scrooge in the world. The only thing which saved you was the generous bonus you gave all of us."

Memories of Sarah in her shapeless suit, glasses and flat heels made a smile tug at the corners of his mouth. He'd remember forever the fire in her eyes at his refusal of her raise. This radiant creature in front of him was a far cry from the Sarah of last May.

"You're not listening to me," Sarah complained.

"I'm sorry—go on. But I still don't want an office party."

Sarah ignored him. "We'll get gifts for everyone and big boxes of candy to take home. It'll be easier to cater the refreshments. And of course, bonuses. Do you think you could increase them a little?"

"I'll have to ask my accounting department about that. Don't forget I have many employees and we've just managed to get into the black."

"I'm sorry, but you didn't do that alone—they all helped."

"I do need you to make me see the whole picture. You can have your increase."

Sarah threw her arms around his neck and gave him a quick kiss to express her gratitude. "Thank you. I promise you'll enjoy this party."

Watching Sarah glow with enthusiasm, Brent was inclined to believe her.

It was Christmas Eve. Carolers had appeared at their doorstep as a very welcome surprise. Aunt Hattie, who was spending the holiday with them, had gone to bed.

The only light in the living room came from the tiny Christmas lights on the tree and the crackling fire.

When Brent sank down on the couch beside her, Sarah stopped thinking about tomorrow's Christmas dinner. It felt so good to spend this quiet time with Brent, regardless of what spring brought.

"I want to give you your gift now," he said. A pleased and expectant expression wreathed his face.

A delicate, filigree gold rose was pinned to the top of a long green velvet box. Sarah opened it with care.

"Oh, oh, it's beautiful." She looked with wonder at the engraved gold chain necklace. Suspended from it was an exquisite amber cameo surrounded by a circle of matched seed pearls. A beautiful woman's profile was carved in the amber. Sarah's finger lightly caressed the cheek of the woman. Warmth seemed to flow from the cameo and into her finger.

"Please put it on me," she whispered.

Brent picked up the necklace with trembling hands. He lowered his head, longing to kiss the hollow in her throat where the pendant would hang. Instead, his hands slid under her hair and he fastened the pearl clasp.

Sarah looked at herself in the mirror over the mantel. The necklace was a live chain of sunshine to warm her heart. She threw her arms around his neck and hugged him tightly.

"A perfect gift, darling. Thank you." She lingered ever so briefly within the circle of his arms.

"I'm glad you're pleased," he said. "A story goes with the pendant."

"Really? Tell me."

"In 1655 a necklace with seven perfectly-matched amber stones was taken from the slain body of the Polish Princess Barbara by Swedish invaders. Somehow, one of the stones slipped off and was hidden by a loyal retainer. It was passed down until a jeweler made the carving of her profile."

"Poor Barbara. But now she has immortality."

Sarah grinned at him. "There's a story with my gift,

too. You have to handle this box with care. Don't tip it."

A red bow was stuck on the lid of a small wooden box with worn leather strips for hinges. Brent raised the lid. Inside, a silver turquoise ring rested on pale yellow desert sand instead of velvet.

"Look at the intricate etching around the stone," Sarah pointed out. "Running Deer—"

"Running Deer? You don't mean for real?"

"Just listen. Yes, Running Deer was the Indian who sold the ring to me. He said the silver is engraved with the symbols of the magic language of his tribe. They bring to the wearer of the ring his heart's desire."

"And you believed him?"

"Of course, You know I want you to have all your desires."

Brent looked at her and yearning filled him. His heart's desire was in front of him. He slipped the ring on his finger. He'd accept all the help he could get, even if it meant believing in this ring.

"I'll believe in the magic." He leaned toward her and lightly kissed her. He wanted to whisper words of love but held back. He didn't want this delightful moment shattered by Sarah's rejection of him. He'd give the ring time to work its magic!

Sarah rose to her feet. "I hate to end a perfect Christmas Eve, but we have an early breakfast and gift-giving in the morning." She placed her hands on his shoulders and kissed him on both cheeks. "Merry Christmas, Brent Chambers."

Brent followed her actions. "Merry Christmas, Mrs. Brent Chambers."

Sarah went up the stairs in a happy daze.

When she got into bed, she thought about the ring.

The ring would grant the wearer his desires. Maybe she should have kept the ring for herself! She had no trouble identifying hers: Brent Chambers as her husband every day. He had been so tender tonight, she forgot their charade.

Besides liking the company and conversation, she was happy to have Aunt Hattie visit during Christmas. When Hattie had revealed the story of the beads, she was so pleased. They had been the last gift of her soldier sweetheart before he left for the battle fields of Europe in the dark days of 1944. He was buried in northern France.

"Oh, how sad." Tears welled up in Sarah's eyes.

"There, there. I've made my peace with my loss and have a very good life. You and my nephew must be sure to value each day you have together."

Sarah turned away from her sharp eyes. Little did Hattie know her days with Brent were limited. Divorce, not death, would end them. Until that time, she would have her hugs, caresses and kisses. Have sweet nothings whispered in her ear, and have her hand held. It sometimes happened even when they didn't hear the warning click of the jet beads! She had her moments of believing it was all real. Sometimes she needed to live in a fool's paradise.

Chapter Twelve

January blahs—a perfect description for what was ailing Sarah. The house looked bare without the holiday decorations. The melting snow and gray skies, with their dark clouds, cast a pall on her world. If only the sun would shine. She'd feel more optimistic about Brent. How was she going to get him to see her as other than a contract wife? Without Aunt Hattie's presence, there was little need to prove they were in love. Henry Stone seemed to have accepted their commitment as true.

Sarah wished she could have her brother come to visit. However, she didn't think she could fool him long. And she didn't want her family to know she had married basically for money. Now she knew it wasn't the main reason but the contract told another story.

She was so tired of lies and secrets. She still hadn't told Brent about her old apartment. Since there was no reason to flee from Aunt Hattie, she hadn't gone back to it. She should stop wasting her money on the rent, but low self-confidence made her hold on to it, just in case.

162

The holidays had enabled Sarah to put Ashley out of her mind, but now her specter haunted her again. She was still in the city she said she hated. Sarah read the newspapers to learn what she was doing. She would have shouted with joy if there had been an engagement announcement, but no such luck.

What *had* happened in Dallas? If there were any more secret meetings, she didn't know when. Brent was home in the evening and on the weekends. During office hours? That was a possibility, but Sarah shrank from such a sordid thought. Still, what did she really know about the inner thoughts of a man who could marry—*marry*—a woman for financial reasons only? Have a signed marriage contract with a specific time span and a planned ending in divorce? Her role in his life was fake and make-believe.

At five o'clock in the afternoon Sarah looked outside. The snowflakes were large, coming fast and furious. In no time every tree, twig and bush had a furry covering. Already, the skies were darkening. Tearing her gaze from the wonderland in her garden, Sarah observed the way the cars crawled past the house. The roads must be very slick and treacherous.

She hoped Brent had had the sense to leave the office early. She leaned closer to the window, her nose touching the cold glass. When a car's headlights swung into the circular driveway, she hurried to meet Brent at the door.

Heedless of the wet snow covering his shoulders, Sarah's welcoming kiss on his lips was warm and lingering. At Brent's look of surprise, she stammered, "I—I was worried about you. I imagined you in a ditch and even dead!"

Brent gave a laugh and hugged her. Rare moments

such as this were treasured by him. Someday, they would be the norm, not the exception.

Dinner was a happy affair. They laughed and conversed easily. Brent had fallen into the practice of bringing Sarah up-to-date on the condition of his business. He found it soothing to talk to her about his work and to listen to her astute suggestions. He never failed to admire her quick grasp of a situation. She was all a husband wanted at the end of a day.

After dessert, Sarah raised her coffee cup. She toasted, "Here's to the nicest snowfall of the year."

"Here, here."

"Don't you love walking in the snow? I recall vividly my parents waking my brother and me and getting us dressed so we could walk in a new snow like this one. It's one of the dearest memories of my childhood."

Brent shrugged his shoulders. "I never did. Uncle Matthew and I wouldn't think to do so."

Sarah thought his childhood sounded very bleak. Yet, Brent spoke of his uncle with affection and acted as though he had had a normal upbring. Tonight she wanted him to have memories of their first walk in the snow.

She took his hand.

"Come, walk with me. You need to start a book of memories with me."

Brent was reading the newspaper, comfortable in his leather wing-backed chair. The beautiful snow of three days ago was no longer a welcome sight. It was a slushy, icy mess. He was glad to be home. When Sarah took the paper out of his grasp and tossed it aside, he was startled.

"What do you—"

Her answer was to grab his hand and start pulling him to his feet. "I'd like you to drive me to the shopping mall. I'm in the mood for a big ice cream cone."

"Ice cream? Are you crazy? Look outside. The driving is terrible and the weather isn't the ice cream kind."

"Oh, come on. You're a good driver. I really, really want one. Don't you want one, too?"

"A cone? I haven't had one since I was a kid."

"Honestly? Not since you were young? Then it's time you did. These are delicious, soft ice cream cones. You haven't lived until you taste one."

"I'll take a raincheck."

She looked at his hard, uncompromising expression. The dimple in her cheek deepened and her lips curved up. Throwing her arms around his neck, she rained kisses all over his face. "Please, please, please, Brent, my darling, my precious, my adorable—"

Brent threw up his hands. "All right, all right. I'll take you to the mall." No way could he refuse such a wonderful assault on his person. If only Sarah did it more often.

The drive was made safely and in a short time they were eating ice cream.

When the cones were finished, she solemnly handed him several paper napkins.

"Thank you. Better late than never, I presume?"

Sarah linked her arm through his. "Come. Let's go window shopping. You can add tonight to your memories. Remember we did this on our honeymoon."

He couldn't remember ever having had such a carefree evening in his life. Sarah . . . could he part with her at the end of their year? He wished he knew whether she was acting all the time. He hope not.

The sky was a clear blue; the cold air, crisp; the chickadees sang a loud song. Sarah opened her window and listened to the birds. To honor Valentine's Day, she wore a red sweater and a short, black miniskirt. Would it catch Brent's eye?

She picked up his gift and gave it to him before he left for the office.

She watched him tear away the wrapping she had spent so much time on, paying no attention to the "I love you's" printed on the white stripes. It was so hard to buy Brent a gift. An I.D. bracelet with his initials on it was her choice. She had the jeweler engrave on the back two connected hearts with their initials in them. Had she been foolish to let him see she wanted this marriage to be forever, two hearts beating as one? If this wasn't what he wanted, he could just tease her for being romantic on Valentine's Day.

"Wow." When he held the bracelet to the light and admired the engraving of his initials, she knew she had picked a good gift. She held her breath as he looked inside and saw the hearts.

Brent gave a low laugh and swept her into his arms and off her feet, yearning to hold her all the Valentine Days in the future. His lips covered hers, tenderly and gently.

He slowly set her back on her feet and held out his wrist. "Will you do the honors?" He admired it again. He reached into his pocket. "This is for you, Sweetheart. Happy Valentine's Day." He was happy for the occasion to call Sarah by all the endearing terms he longed to use. He was safe today.

The small box had red paper. On the top was pinned a delicate gold heart with Cupid's arrow piercing it.

"How exquisite!" A pair of earrings were in the box. A diamond was in the center of the heart. Three gold chains of graduated lengths hung from it and had a small diamond heart at the end.

Sarah hurried to the hall mirror and put them on. The hearts sparkled as they swayed below her ears.

"Oh, I love them." Reaching up, she pulled his head down and kissed him. "I'm going to wear them all day."

He stared at her, drinking in her loveliness. She seemed to become more beautiful each day. Or dared he hope it was the inner radiance of love shining through?

"Wear them tonight when I take you out to dinner."

The I.D. bracelet slid down Brent's wrist from under the white cuff of his shirt sleeve, and the hearts in Sarah's earings swung to-and-fro. They circled slowly around the dance floor at the country club. Brent dared to hold her tightly to him, fitting her soft curves to his. "I could dance all night," Sarah murmured.

As though he read her mind, Brent whirled her around the tall, potted plants at the edge of the ballroom. He pressed his lips to hers until the music stopped. They stayed in each other's embrace until it started again.

Ashley was at the dance accompanied by a tall man with graying hair. They had exchanged greetings before Brent skillfully danced them to another part of the floor. Sarah put her out of her mind and floated on a cloud of happiness on a perfect, romantic evening.

* * *

Although Valentine's Day was in the past, its heart-stopping overture played on, recalled by Sarah two months later. Rare romantic occasions like that gave Sarah hope that she and Brent were nearer to making their make-believe marriage a real one.

These thoughts were interfering with her attempt to complete one of her term papers, not to mention her concern about three tests she had coming up. How quickly time was flying by. Last September, the end of the school year was in the distant mists of the future. But, in a blink, she was facing her final exams and handing in the last of her term papers. Soon, she'd have the coveted degree in her hand.

She was determined to make A's in all of her courses. She wasn't worried, she always competed against herself. This year she wanted Brent to be proud of her, which was a much greater stimulus.

The knock on her sitting room door interrupted her concentration.

"Come in." She turned in her desk chair.

Brent sauntered in and smiled at her. "You look busy."

"You know how it is with us bookworms."

"I hope your schedule is flexible."

"Depends."

"I promised to take you with me if I went back to Dallas. I have to go the day after tomorrow. I'd like you to go with me."

"Oh, no," Sarah wailed. "I have two tests that day and another one, the next day. Can't you go later in the week?"

"Sorry. I have to be in Dallas on Wednesday. Aren't there make-up tests if you miss the exam?"

"I don't want to do that. It would be scheduled weeks from now and I might not get the A's I've been hoping for."

A surge of annoyance swept over Brent—getting an A was more important than being with him in Dallas? She sure put him in his place.

"Another time, then." Brent hid his disappointment and pain in his light tone.

"Are you sure you can't postpone your trip by three days? What's so important about it?"

"The arrangements were made weeks ago. An important paint supplier has the amounts I need, at a price I can afford. When I have to buy large quantities, money is still a problem. At least until May."

"I always wanted to see Dallas. I'm going to miss you."

The unexpected tears filling her eyes touched him. His annoyance gone, he tried to console her.

"It's only for three days. And there will be other trips, I promise."

After Brent left, Sarah worked on her term paper and studied for her exams. In the middle of her notes on Advanced Accounting, she found herself thinking of his trip to Dallas. Was he meeting Ashley? She was still lingering in Brighton.

Her enthusiasm for studying evaporated. She was no longer interested in the results—A's didn't seem so impressive anymore. She should have gone with Brent and taken the make-up tests. Now, when it was too late, she had such wisdom!

Her doubts and fears nagged her. She couldn't call his hotel room. If Ashley answered as before—no, it would be unbearable. She had to trust Brent.

Still she had to know about Ashley.

Instead of making the call to Brent's suite, she called Ashley's apartment. She would ask the date of the spring festival of the Brighton Hospital board of which Ashley was chairperson.

A heavily accented voice answered the phone. A vacuum cleaner hummed noisily in the background.

"Yes, yes, Ms. Ashley is in . . . What? Yes, I just told you where she is."

Sarah's fears had been verified. Though indistinct, she was sure the maid had said Ashley was in Dallas. She sat limply on her chair. No wonder Brent hadn't tried to change her mind. Her past doubts rose to torment her. All those times Brent worked late . . . but as before, there was nothing she could do about it. But that fact didn't make her feel any better.

Thursday night Sarah, in spite of all her good intentions, moped by the phone. She didn't expect a call. Before the first ring ended, she picked it up.

"Brent!" she cried happily. "How are you? Did you get your contract? When are you—"

"Whoa. All is okay here. How are you and your tests?"

"Everything is fine here. I think I made A's." She paused and added, "The house is empty without you."

"This hotel room isn't like home either."

"Tell me—"

"Just a minute. There's someone at the door."

In the distance Sarah heard the murmur of a conversation. A woman's soft laugh was cut off.

"Sorry, Sarah, but I have to go. I'll be home tomorrow afternoon on flight 424. Good night."

Sarah slowly put down the phone. Ashley. It could be no one else. Sarah didn't want to be melodramatic, but it felt like her heart was breaking. It was a physical, hurting pain.

The next morning, Sarah tried to put all thoughts of what was happening in Dallas out of her mind. While sorting through her mail an envelope from her bank caught her attention. From the looks of it, it had been sent to the wrong address before finally coming to her. The postmark was April second. Today was the sixteenth.

In January she had agreed to Brent's suggestion that he deposit her monthly payment directly into her account. She had been grateful for his thoughtfulness. It had been traumatic each month for her to see it on her dresser, a monthly reminder of their fake marriage. The flowers helped, but not enough. Without the check to deposit, it was so much easier to delude herself about her part in his life.

If only there weren't so many ups and downs in their relationship. At times, she was wildly happy because she was sure Brent was falling in love with her. Then, there was today: down in the depths of despair, being eaten up with jealousy and unhappiness.

At first, she barely read the deposit slip—then she looked at it again. She leaned back in her chair and closed her eyes.

Brent had deposited all the money due to her through May. She was paid in full. Brent's financial obligations to her were fulfilled.

Sarah was puzzled. Why had he done this? Was this his way to remind her, in a gentle way, that their marriage of convenience was over? That she had time to gradually wind up her affairs and start making plans for her future, alone? It had to be.

A few minutes ago, she thought she had hit rock

bottom in her feelings. Wrong, wrong, wrong. She felt greater depths of despair and unhappiness today. The date of the bank deposit told the story. He must have made his plans to go to Dallas and meet with Ashley.

He had known all about her tests. She clearly remembered telling him about them, and he had teased her about wanting the best grades. Of course, he never thought his wife would go with him, especially since she was intent on making top marks. He was just covering all his bases. He was so good at charades.

He couldn't wait for the end of the contract year to be over with Ashley. But he had to do it secretly in order to get the rest of his inheritance. Hadn't he just told her money was still a problem in his business?

Sarah covered her face with her hands as tears streamed down her cheeks. Fool, fool, fool! She didn't want to remember Brent's warm kisses or the shelter of his strong arms. All this time he had been seeing his childhood sweetheart, had loved only Ashley . . .

Having faced reality, Sarah stoically dried her tears. She had to think. She had signed a contract for one year and was still willing to abide by its terms. How clearly she remembered Brent promising to be the perfect husband.

Heartbroken, she no longer felt obligated to stay with him. She wasn't going to live in his house another minute. She could not ignore this trip as she had done the first one. No more acting the loving wife before an audience. He had even made it easy for her by depositing the rest of the money due her. This money was hers and she was going to keep it. She had *earned* it. Well, when he came home from Dallas, she wouldn't be here. She was through being taken advantage of. She didn't care if she was being fair or unfair.

Brent could say she had a family emergency and was called to the bedside of her father until May fifteenth. He'd collect his inheritance and the deed to his house. He could then sue for divorce on the grounds of desertion.

In spite of her pain and unhappiness, Sarah wanted Brent to collect his inheritance. She couldn't live with herself if her actions caused him to lose everything at this late date. He had done nothing this year to really hurt her. She had no reason to expect a contract husband to be faithful. She had set herself up to fall by spinning fantasies and dreams. Founded on sand, they crumbled. Brent probably had no idea she loved him. Not that she had ever told him . . . it was a good thing she had kept her love a secret.

Sarah quickly packed two bags. Later, she'd think about getting the rest of her belongings. When she placed the engagement ring and the necklace in an envelope on Brent's bureau, the tears flowed again. She dashed them aside, vowing never to cry another tear. She had been so foolish. Brent had been very explicit about the terms of their marriage. She should have listened.

After ordering a taxi, she called Symes to her room.

"Please take these bags downstairs. A taxi will be here shortly."

"Mrs. Sarah, are you going somewhere? Why can't I drive you?"

"No, thank you. This is a family emergency. I've left a letter for Brent."

Before calling Symes, she had written a letter to Brent. She didn't want him to follow her, and neither did she want him to call the police to report her missing.

The wording of the letter was terrible but the message was clear.

> *Brent,*
>
> *I can't go on with this sham of a marriage, not after what has happened in Dallas. Please don't try to find me. Tell the others that my father is ill and I've gone home. You can pretend to call and learn I have to stay home until May fifteenth. You can then collect your inheritance and sue for divorce. I won't hinder you in any way. I'll be in touch after the end of our contract.*

When she came out of the house, Symes was stowing the bags into the taxi. He tried once more, "Please, let me—"

"Not this time. Thanks for everything and tell the others thank you also. Goodbye."

She quickly got into the cab and gave the address of her old apartment. She had been so smart to keep it. She knew now why she had never found the right time to tell Brent about it: she'd never been able to shake the fear that her marriage wasn't going to have a fairytale ending.

When she looked back at the house through the rear window of the cab, tears filled her eyes. She was saying goodbye to her home, the place where she had spent some of the happiest months of her life.

Tears fell in earnest. Brent was forever lost to her. Her heart was truly breaking, but her life would go on. Somehow, she would find the courage to finish her college year—to have at least *one* dream come true. She'd be economically secure because of her degree. For this, she would be eternally grateful to Brent. For her broken heart, he bore no responsibility.

Chapter Thirteen

Brent looked around the airport waiting area. No Sarah. He had been sure she would be here. Oh, well. He'd be home soon.

Home. A wondrous place. Anticipation and happiness surged through him, and he owed it all to Sarah. Marrying her had brought true love into his life.

During the flight Brent decided to stop pussyfooting around. He had wasted months holding back and not telling Sarah he had fallen in love with her.

Surely he hadn't misread the look in her eyes. Surely his shy, darling wife was waiting for him to declare his love, to prove to her this was no longer a marriage of convenience. That it was a true marriage, after all.

As soon as he saw her, he was going to take her in his arms and pour out his love for her. To beg her, on bended knee, to be his real wife in every way.

He had to tell her today.

He opened the door to his house and called, "Sarah, my darling, I'm home." All his heart was in this greeting. Only silence met him. He called again, more urgently, "Sarah, darling!"

Mrs. Ames hurried toward him, her hands twisting the corner of her apron into a ball.

"Mrs. Sarah's not here. I don't know where she is. She packed two suitcases, called a taxi and left at eleven o'clock."

"What? Sarah's left? What did she say? What—"

"I didn't see her go. You'll have to ask Symes. Here he comes."

Symes said, "She told me it was a family emergency and that she had left a letter for you."

"Of course, only a family emergency would make Sarah leave in such a hurry. I'll go and read the letter. Don't worry," he told the servants, "I'll let you know what happened."

Brent took the stairs two at a time. The letter was propped up against his dresser mirror. When he pulled out the letter, the ring and the necklace tumbled out. Brent's spirits plummeted at the sight. He sat on the edge of his bed and read the letter. He read it again, trying to absorb the message. Trying to understand what she said. What did Sarah think he was doing in Dallas that would drive her away? He just bought some paint—what was wrong with that? He shook his head.

He read the rest of the letter. Her father wasn't ill. He was supposed to tell this story as a cover-up for the reason she left and wouldn't be coming back to the house. She still wanted him to get his inheritance—and a divorce. She hadn't said one word about caring for him or that she was sorry to leave. She hadn't even signed the letter.

Brent felt numb. The most important words of the

letter were "I can't go on with this sham of a marriage." Sarah didn't love him, had never loved him.
He had been deluding himself.

Where was she now? Though she didn't love him,
his love for her was real. He wanted to know she was
safe. He had to talk to her, face-to-face, and have her
explain what was so wrong that she had to leave without seeing him. Suddenly a jealous thought occurred
to him. Johnny. The other man in Sarah's past. The
man she had gone to see on two separate occasions.
No, it couldn't be. Somehow, he couldn't believe this
of Sarah. She was too honorable; she'd lived up to the
terms of their agreement in every way. She thought
something had happened in Dallas, and it had driven
her away. He had to find her and make things right.

When Brent went downstairs, Mrs. Ames and Symes were still in the hall, waiting to receive the news.
They were very fond of Sarah and he had to relieve
their worry. He smiled.

"Nothing to worry about. Sarah's father isn't well
and she felt she should go home and check on him.
I'll be calling her later."

How easily the lies came. He and Sarah had had
lots of practice. Soon, they would speak only the truth.

Brent went into his study and closed the door. He
paced the floor. What to do first? He didn't think Sarah
had gone to her family. Even though she no longer
wanted to live with him, she didn't want him to lose
all they had worked to achieve. Only a month to go
and it would all be his, the money and the house. But
without Sarah, it meant nothing to him. He'd gladly
lose it all if only she would come back to him.

He put his head in his hands. Why had he waited

so long to tell her he loved her, had loved from the first time he laid eyes on her? Why had it taken so long to realize that this marriage of convenience was only to bring him closer to his true love? He had to find her!

Helplessness almost overwhelmed him. He knew so little about her past. It was a good thing he didn't run his business in the way he'd been conducting his personal life. How do you find a person who's left no clue? How quickly his stable world had been overturned and his happiness destroyed. He had been so confident coming home today, knowing that he was going to make things right. His trip had seemed so important he couldn't postpone it so Sarah could come with him. How pointless it all seemed now. Sarah was worth everything to him.

At least he didn't have to worry that Sarah had been kidnapped and was being held for ransom. She had left of her own accord. She was somewhere safe but miles away from him. Evidently, she couldn't stand to be with him for another month. A knife thrust in his heart would have felt like this.

How he missed her. He had been a fool not to tell her how much he loved her. But, he argued, there *was* a good reason to keep silent. As he had requested, she was only pretending to care for him. If he had expressed his feelings, she would have accused him of breaking the terms of their agreement—especially her clause about abuse. He had been afraid she'd walk out on him if he became amorous. Well, now she had done just that, and he might never have the chance to tell her his true feelings.

Before he called in a private investigator to find her, Brent rummaged in his desk for Sarah's personnel folder. He remembered bringing it home from the office. Perhaps there was something there to help him.

Sarah's old address. The place to start.

She may have kept her old apartment. It was logical, since their marriage was supposed to last only a year. She had enough money to keep paying the rent on it.

Brent found a parking place in front of the apartment building on Fairview Street. Located on a quiet street, the building was an old-fashioned brownstone with a wide stoop.

Not knowing why she ran off without a word of explanation, he didn't want to alert Sarah. He pushed a random doorbell. Fortunately for him, the tenant buzzed the door open without question. He slipped into the foyer and looked at the mailboxes. Gordan was #3-D.

He walked up the stairs. The small name plate on the door read "Johnny Lennox/Sarah Gordan." Brent's heart sank. Here was tangible proof of his fears. Wasn't it common to live with someone without the benefit of marriage? Had Sarah?

Brent started to turn away. No, he was here and he needed to talk to Sarah. Johnny, if he was in the apartment, could take a hike! She had signed a contract with him, and, by golly, he was going to hold her to it to the very last day.

Brent could feel his temper rising and his knock on the door was loud.

He raised his fist to knock again. The door swung open and Sarah stood before him. He was so glad to see she was safe he almost crushed her into his arms. Her expressionless face and cold eyes stopped him.

"Please don't bother me. I—"

He pushed past her and entered the room, glancing

around quickly. Sarah was alone. He breathed a sigh of relief.

"I don't care what you want. I demand an explanation—and a darn good one—for running away like this." He glared at her.

Sarah shrugged her shoulders and sat down on the lone easy chair. He took a seat on the matching sofa, noting the worn slip covers. He waited for her to speak.

"I couldn't take it anymore. Your trip to Dallas was the last straw."

"I asked you to go with me."

"Yes, and you're such an accomplished liar. Come on! You wanted to be with Ashley again."

"What are you talking about? I wasn't with Ashley. Where did you get that crazy idea?"

"I called her apartment and her maid said she had gone to Dallas—obviously with you! She was in your room the last time you went."

Brent's eyes narrowed into slits as he struggled to control his exasperation. "You've been checking up on me? Are you jealous of Ashley? Last October she was there uninvited, and she left immediately. I was faithful to you then, and on this trip." Brent was thoughtful for a moment. "Are you sure the maid said Dallas? The last time I talked to Ashley she was on her way back to Paris. She's had enough of Brighton."

Sarah's face mirrored her confusion. Paris? Of course. She had heard what she wanted to hear above the noise of the vacuum cleaner and the heavy accent of the maid. Relief almost unnerved her. He had been faithful to her.

Brent knelt before her and took her hands into his

comforting ones. "Do you believe me? I'd never go behind your back. I have no secrets."

Sarah was stricken with guilt and remorse. Brent had no secrets—she did. She covered her face with her hands. She couldn't bear to look into his trusting face. Tears began to trickle between her fingers.

Brent didn't know what to do.

"Sarah, Sarah, what's wrong? What did I say?"

Sarah lifted her tear-streaked face. "Nothing! You didn't do anything. It's me." The tears continued to flow.

Brent pulled her into his arms and stroked her hair. He murmured soothing words until she finally quieted down. He put a finger under her chin and forced Sarah to look at him.

"I'm sure you could never do anything wrong. Tell me and let me be the judge," he urged.

"I should have told you about Johnny. I don't know why I kept putting it off. It never seemed to be the right time. Johnny was my husband. We were married two years ago, but only for six months. He died unexpectedly of a heart attack and I was devasted. We were so happy—"

"My poor darling. Was your grief so great you couldn't talk about it?"

Sarah gazed at him with wonder. How she loved this wonderful, understanding man.

"Oh, Brent, it was terrible. I even went back to using my maiden name and I didn't put it on my employment application." She gave Brent a weary smile. "I'm sorry I didn't tell you."

"You kept this apartment in his memory?"

"Oh, no. I kept it in case our agreement didn't work out. I've made my peace with my past and—"

"And what?"

"I've fallen in love with you and I can't bear to come back to our phony marriage!"

Brent gave a great laugh of joy and hugged her fiercely.

"Sweetheart, I've loved you since the first time I laid eyes on you. I came home today determined to tell you I love you and only you." He kissed her. "Tell me again you love me!"

Sarah hugged him, crying and laughing, "I love you! I've always loved you and thought you never would me. That's why I ran away. I couldn't stay in your house another day with you just pretending to love me. When I saw that you had deposited the rest of my money, I was sure you couldn't wait to get rid of me and return to your first love, Ashley."

"We've wasted almost a year with our foolishnes," Brent said. He kissed her again and urged her toward the door. "Let's go home where we can complete the terms of the will."

Sarah laughed happily. "There are my suitcases. I'm ready to go anywhere with you, my darling husband."

Much later, Brent grinned from ear to ear. The connecting door between the bedrooms was wide open. And next to him was his beautiful, once-elusive Sarah.

"How do you feel now?" he asked.

She stretched slowly like a contented kitten.

"I feel like a much-loved wife. And you?"

He gathered her into his arms. "I feel like your husband. You are my one and only love, my dear Mrs. Chambers."

She whispered, "We'll be tearing up our prenuptial contract, won't we?"

"Yes, but that's for tomorrow. Let's enjoy our first night of true wedded bliss!"